He caught Jessica to his chest, muscular arms wrapped protectively around her. She'd never felt such relief in her life. Suddenly there was a sense of completeness where there had been a huge void.

"What on earth is wrong?"

"The wedding is less than nine hours away, my work crew just canceled and I can't even begin to tell you what's at stake today. I know I don't deserve it, but if you'll help me, Drew, I promise I'll explain everything tomorrow."

He smiled, dimple and all, and guided her to the sidewalk.

"Let me make a couple of phone calls. I'll meet you in the Commons in five minutes."

He ran his hand down the back of her hair as she turned to walk away.

A glance over her shoulder sent a thrill of hope through her heart. He was still watching, tenderness etched in his features.

MAE NUNN

grew up in Houston and graduated from the University of Texas with a degree in communications. When she fell for a transplanted Englishman who lived in Atlanta, Mae hung up her spurs to become a Southern belle. Today she and her husband make their home with their two children in Georgia. Mae has been with a major air-express company for twenty-five years, currently serving as a regional customer service manager. She began writing four years ago. When asked how she felt about being part of the Steeple Hill family, Mae summed her response up with one word, "Yeeeeeha!"

HEARTS IN BLOOM

MAE NUNN

Published by Steeple Hill Books™

STEEPLE HILL BOOKS

Steeple
Hill®

ISBN 0-373-87264-X

HEARTS IN BLOOM

Copyright © 2004 by Mae Nunn

Printed in U.S.A.

Chapter One

D_{irt.}

There was just something so appealing about dirt.

Jessica Holliday couldn't remember a time in her twenty-six years when she hadn't been fascinated by the stuff and the miracles it generated. She breathed deeply of its comforting smell and lightly massaged the site of her knee injury.

Atlanta's top orthopedic surgeon had performed the anterior medialization, grafting bone and marrow, inserting titanium screws and closing the knee with thirty-five staples. But no amount of medical skill would ever restore full strength to her leg.

A small price to pay, considering Adam Crockett was lost forever to his grieving family. A family who blamed her for his death.

At least she had the chance to start again. She'd planned better than her mother, who'd ended up with no education and a child to support after her ex-military husband had abandoned them. Thanks to a green thumb and a very tight budget, Jessica had learned something besides dance. She could design, plant and tend gardens of all kinds, and the proof covered the ten-acre campus of Sacred Arms.

Sitting cross-legged in the shade of six-foot-high fuchsia and white azalea bushes, she admired the beds in bloom. Tall clusters of purple iris and feathery, light pink plumes of astilbe surrounded her. Fragrant bunches of lavender waved in the warm spring breeze.

An afternoon sun glinted through the shady gardens of the town-home complex and she ducked her head to avoid the momentary brightness. Her downcast eyes were drawn to her hands, to the nails that were in desperate need of a manicure. The fashionable mid-town salon had probably figured out months ago that she wouldn't be keeping her regular appointment any longer.

She'd kept her nails maintained only out of responsibility anyway, hating the busy metallic clicking of the clippers and the rough filing and the smell of acrylic. But a principal performer for the Atlanta Dance Theater could hardly greet supporters with soil under her fingernails. Now the trace of dirt beneath her short nails was a welcome sight.

How quickly priorities could change. One moment she had been navigating the dark highway, the next she'd been blinded by the overhead lights of the operating room.

From where she sat, Jessica had a clear view of the security gate. It swung open to admit a fancy white sedan that pulled a little too quickly into the parking lot. That could mean only one thing. Valentine was late to meet a prospective buyer.

With the always immaculately dressed real estate agent close by, Jessica paused to consider her own attire. She surveyed the baggy sweat suit, stained with everything from mulch to mustard. She needed new clothes desperately, but refused to acknowledge the result of her sixty-pound weight gain in such a permanent manner.

From outside the gates, a sports car's too-loud engine growled. A shiny blue car glided to a stop beside the sidewalk and a hulk of a man rose from the car and stepped into the sunshine. Standing ramrod straight, he surveyed the community of private town houses. With an arm raised to shield his eyes against the glare, he appeared to salute.

Jessica scoffed at the memory it evoked. Her worthless father had teased her mother with a similar gesture on the rare occasions when he'd meandered through their lives. The braided rug beside Jessica's childhood bed had worn thin where she'd knelt. Prayers for her father to stay with them had gone unanswered, so she'd given up on prayer altogether.

She wagged her head to shake off the daydreaming,

a thick ponytail swishing about the neck of her shirt, and swiped at her forehead with a dirty hand.

With an aluminum cane tucked beneath her arm, she returned to the task of fertilizing the prizewinning azaleas. She scooted backward across the grass to the next spot needing attention, eased over, careful to avoid the still-mending leg, and returned to work.

Drew Keegan had emerged from the shady interior of his perfectly restored '67 fastback into the afternoon sun. He stood, hand raised to block the glare, admiring the grounds of Sacred Arms. In many ways the property, located in the historic Grant Park district of Atlanta, still had the look of the 1920s Christian school it had once been.

"Very interesting." He spoke aloud to himself.

Making the scene even more interesting, the same white luxury car that had blown past him on the interstate was now pulled to the curb farther inside the gate.

The driver swiveled to the left, extending shapely legs. She offered an appealing view of cream-colored stockings that led to a fashionably short, pale pink linen skirt.

Just as he realized the long, low whistle came from his own lips, the matching pink jacket appeared and above it a charming face, sporting a devilish smile.

"Dahhhlin'! You must be Drew. How sweet of you to make a pass at a woman old enough to be your mama."

The woman was actually old enough to be his grandmama, but she'd probably never look it as long as there were good plastic surgeons in Georgia.

"Ms. Chandler?" Drew had a terrible suspicion that he was blushing, something he'd rarely done in his adult life. "Please accept my apology, ma'am. I don't know what possessed me to do such a thing."

"Oh, honey, you couldn't help yourself. I've always had that effect on handsome young men."

Realizing she was quite serious, he accepted that he was excused for having no control over his own actions and reached to shake the brightly jeweled hand she offered.

"I appreciate you meeting me so late in the afternoon, Ms. Chandler."

"Please call me Valentine, and it's no problem at all. Besides, Sacred Arms is so beautiful this time of day, don't you agree?" She extended her right arm in a sweeping gesture, as if presenting the property for his approval.

The sun played off the colorful Tennessee fieldstone, producing every shade of brown, gold and orange. Fighting for attention were the beautifully restored stained-glass windows that had been painstakingly assembled three quarters of a century earlier. The enduring images of Christ welcoming little children, blessing the fishes and loaves, talking with the woman at the well and praying at the garden at Gethsemane glowed beneath the warm rays.

Father, could Your will for my life be any more

obvious? Thank You for guiding me to this special place, he silently prayed.

Drew let his gaze wander from the structure that had been the chapel and sweep the rest of the spacious compound. There were four primary buildings that had been converted into living space. The fifth, containing an extraordinary copper-domed rotunda, was what Valentine had described over the phone as the Commons.

"I know it's warm out here and you'd like to visit the models, but let's just take a minute to walk around back so you can see the gardens. A good friend of mine, a precious girl, really, grows the most amazing plants in this old red clay."

They approached a waist-high stone wall. Behind it, a bright bed of tall azaleas graciously set off the gray river rock. As they rounded the end of the wall, his eye caught some movement beneath the blossoms.

Expecting to see a house pet enjoying a roll in the grass, he was surprised to witness the grass-stained backside of a woman slowly emerge as she scooted precariously out of the bushes on her hands and one knee. Her left hand clutched a bag of fertilizer spikes. Her right hand reached for a cane.

"Jessica, dahhhlin', there you are. Come and meet the gentleman who's about to buy a home here."

Trained for years to embody grace, Jessica found herself in the most ungraceful position of her life. She stopped her backward crawl, face pointed toward the foliage, back end toward the unexpected visitors, and ground her teeth at the unwanted interruption. With her damaged knee, rising quickly to recover from the embarrassing introduction was simply not an option. She folded her good leg beneath her, dropped to her hip and turned to face them.

Smiling down at her from a towering height was one of the biggest men she'd ever seen. No doubt the guy was part of a major football team's defensive line. She didn't mean to give him the once-over, but from her position she couldn't help but take him in from the bottom up.

Expensive loafers peeked from beneath well-tailored khakis. His chest and shoulders were broad, arms well developed, neck thick and jaw very square. A silly Rhett Butler mustache twitched above a smiling mouth, while warm hazelnut eyes clashed with military-issue, close-cropped dark brown hair.

"Ms. Jessica Holliday, may I introduce Captain Andrew Keegan. He just moved here from Virginia and is hoping to make Sacred Arms his new home. Jessica, Drew was a Green Beret."

Oh, great, Rambo for a neighbor!

The judgment must have shown on her face. His smile disappeared, stealing with it the slight dimple in his left cheek. But the intense look in his eyes never changed. He glanced from her face down to the cane and back again.

"It's a pleasure to meet you." He leaned from the waist and offered her his hand.

She took it and they shook briefly. When she tried

to release his strong grip, he held fast, an offer to support her weight if she wanted to stand. She considered staying where she was, but decided the disadvantage of her present position was worse than accepting help.

He maintained their grip as she reached for the cane. He squatted, taking a firm hold on her right elbow with his left hand. Fixing her eyes upon his, she nodded, a signal to stand. With him as the anchor she rose to her full height, taking care to lean on her right leg gently until the aluminum support was planted firmly at her side.

Drew took in every nuance of the effort, along with the rest of her, as well as he could without appearing to be completely without manners for the second time that hour.

She was much taller than he'd expected, with a full figure, although it was difficult to tell much about her shape under her rumpled, ill-fitting clothes. Beneath the smudges of red clay she had clear, fair skin. She was pink from the sun or the exertion or possibly embarrassment.

Her makeup-free eyes held a familiar glare. He couldn't quite make out what she was telling him with it. He knew only they were the most enchanting shade of emerald he'd ever seen. He was tempted to remove the sprig of hedge perched in the bangs that were many shades of blond.

She snatched her hand free.

Defiance. That was the look. He'd seen it so many

times in the eyes of new recruits that he should have recognized it immediately.

"Jessica, honey, I believe these purple delphiniums are gonna be even more spectacular than last year. If that's possible," Valentine observed.

"I think you may be right. But it's probably because they've had so much more attention this season." As she spoke to Valentine, Drew noticed that Jessica rubbed her hand on a stained pant leg, cleaning off any traces of his touch.

"Are you the groundskeeper here?" he inquired.

"I suppose that's what I am now." She glanced at her dirty nails and back again.

"You must have help." He could tell from the way her eyes narrowed she'd taken the comment as an insult. "I mean, it's such a large campus, so much variety. It would be hard for anybody to tend all this alone."

Her chin jutted forward at the observation.

"I'm stronger than I look right now," she insisted, "but I always manage to find some willing hands for the heavy stuff. A service details the lawn, but it's all under my direction. I've intentionally put in lots of perennials, and the rock garden takes care of itself."

"Sugar, don't you dare downplay the miracles you've done with this place." Valentine stepped close and looped her arm through Jessica's, linking spotless linen with grimy fleece.

"Why, you should have seen it before she took over a few years back. The hedges were full of bagworms and there wasn't a flower in sight. What you see now is this sweet child's magic touch.''

Lush green fescue grounds were studded with terra-cotta containers filled with myriad colorful springtime blossoms. With a soft sound, dripping water fell from a Japanese-style bamboo fountain into a small shallow pond. Freestanding island beds gave the illusion of space even in the angular corner of the property. She'd carved out kaleidoscopes edged in rough stone and large boulders.

Nodding his approval, Drew appreciated the extraordinary breadth of knowledge along with the eye for design and balance it must have taken to produce such an inviting place.

''My mother would have been jealous,'' he said. ''She didn't have the touch herself and could never find hired help capable of producing anything quite like this.''

Jessica bristled at the compliment. He wondered for the millionth time in his life why it was so hard to find the right thing to say to a woman.

''Thank you,'' Jessica muttered. ''I think.''

Drew admired the creeping ivy on the rock wall, pretending to miss the annoyance in her voice. He turned to face her, smiling once again, and extended his hand.

''It was nice meeting you.''

''My pleasure. And welcome to Sacred Arms,'' Jessica replied without warmth. She looked as if she hoped his credit was bad.

"I'm so glad we ran into you, dahhhlin'," Valentine interjected. "You're getting around beautifully. It's obvious that your little physical therapist is doing you a world of good."

Before Jessica could respond, a yapping ball of white hair came racing down the incline, a bright blue leash flying behind it like a superhero's cape. Suddenly the animal sat back on his haunches and threw out all fours as it slammed to a halt against Drew's ankles.

He bent to give full attention to the pup as it quickly recovered, eagerly pawing dirty front feet at recently laundered khakis.

"Hey, buddy, you live around here?" With one hand Drew ruffled short ears covered with long silky hair. With the other he casually but firmly removed the dog's paws from his knees. Too late. The damage was already done. Signs of the animal's afternoon frolic in the spring grass would be on those slacks through numerous launderings.

Jessica half hid a smile behind her hand.

"Oh, I'm sorry. He's mine. Frasier, heel." She spoke the command and pointed to the ground by her left foot. The dog stopped his happy sniffing only long enough to give her a curious glance. Again she snapped her fingers and pointed.

"Frasier! Heel!"

Even though the dog showed no inclination to follow instructions, Drew released the pup's paws so he could obey. Frasier made several quick and surprisingly high jumps, leaving even more stains on the front of Drew's starched khakis.

"Frasier, heel." The male voice was low and calm, but left no doubt who was in control. The little dog responded immediately, made a quick turn and stood at attention by Drew's left heel. "Good boy." The two beamed approval at one another as if they'd practiced the trick a hundred times.

"It figures," Jessica said, annoyed. "I've been working with him for weeks and all he does is run around me in circles. But for a complete stranger, the little traitor behaves like he's just come from the kennel club."

Valentine spoke up. "That little cutie is Jessica's new physical therapist. She's moving around so much better since he came to live with her."

"You mean since he showed up on my doorstep and refused to leave, don't you?"

Her tone implied aggravation, but the look she gave the hairy pup said otherwise.

She gestured toward Drew's slacks. "I'm really sorry about your pants," she said, struggling to contain a smirk.

"I'm an old pro in the laundry room." He shrugged and brushed at the marks.

"I never mastered that area myself," she admitted.

Drew bent toward the waiting dog, collected the blue leash, handed it to her with a smile and said, "Somehow that doesn't surprise me."

* * *

Jessica climbed the hill slowly, but faster than she had a month ago. Frasier really had helped. His constant demands for attention had forced her out of survivor guilt mode, off the couch and back into the sunshine. Back to the gardens, where she couldn't resist the call of crabgrass. It was like a siren, tempting her to bend, reach, pull and then to find a way to gather up the mess and haul it away.

Like most able-bodied people, she'd taken the ability to perform those simple tasks for granted. Not anymore. Valentine said Jessica was blessed, but if that meant losing your career and killing a man in the process, God could keep His blessings.

As Frasier tugged at the leash, urging her on, she turned her face upward, enjoying the sun on her cheeks. The warmth suddenly deepened as she realized Rambo could still be watching. Just as quickly, she shrugged off the thought. Why would a handsome guy give her a second glance? And even if he did, the view from where he stood was certainly not much to see.

She snorted laughter at her own cruel joke. There was plenty to see. In this red sweat suit she must resemble the broad side of a barn.

Drew couldn't resist watching as she trudged slowly up the incline. Red had always been his favorite color. Even filthy, it was perfect with her fair complexion and those challenging eyes.

"That precious girl has been through a lot in the past few months. But she's a fighter."

He turned his attention to the older woman. "I noticed."

"Shall we get on up to the models? I know you're anxious to see our homes."

"I'd like that. And thank you for showing me the gardens. Everything I heard is true—they are magnificent."

Taking the lead, Valentine sashayed up the long stone path, putting one small, fashionable pump in front of the other.

"Well, they're a real source of pride. The landscaping is a special touch we think adds so much to the beauty of the property. We considered replacing the vegetable beds with a basketball goal."

She waved her hand in that direction and sunlight danced off the many diamonds on her fingers and wrist. "But most of our residents objected. They enjoy the option to hoe a row of their own if they like, and Jess keeps the older folks up to their elbows in tomatoes and summer squash. Why, that girl can fling cantaloupe guts into her compost heap and accidentally grow melon better than anything that was planted on purpose."

She tilted her platinum head back and smiled up at him in a beguiling way. "You'll see."

They reached the formal terrace and took a path lined with yellow-leaved hostas.

"Let me show you the three-bedroom model,

Drew, honey. I'm certain this is exactly what you're looking for," Valentine said as she fitted the key into the lock. She swung the door wide and stepped aside.

He fell for the high ceilings, red oak floors, stark white walls and old-fashioned louvered windows in less time than it took to rotate a set of tires.

"Would you mind if we went to your office now?"

"Drew, dahhhlin', we can do whatever you like," she murmured agreeably.

She led him toward the end of the common hallway. Valentine stepped carefully around a bag of potting soil that had tipped over and spilled out onto the otherwise spotless floor. She appeared not even to notice, much less mind.

A door stood wide open and pop music, mingled with excited yapping, flowed from inside. He felt like a snoop for peering in as they passed, but he was naturally curious about his new neighbors.

Where the empty unit he'd just seen had appealed to him in its monochromatic, uncluttered state, this one couldn't have been more different, more colorful or more alive with…stuff.

From behind a wall of potted ficus trees, a blur of white fur flashed into view, triumphantly dragging an empty plastic tray that had once held bedding plants. In an instant the plastic was forgotten. The animal charged the doorway.

"Hey, buddy, we meet again." Drew squatted to accept the greeting.

The pup stood on its hind legs with front paws

perched atop Drew's knee. Drew scratched the length of its back while it arched appreciatively and broke into a big doggie smile, pink tongue lolling to one side.

"He is the worst excuse for a guard dog that I have ever seen!" Jessica complained.

"Nobody said he was supposed to save your life. Just get you out for a walk once in a while," a female voice farther inside replied.

Jessica was followed by what Drew could have sworn was a caftan-clad ringer for the lead singer of the Mamas & the Papas, the late Cass Elliott.

"Frasier, who's your little friend?" Mama Cass smiled down at Drew.

Valentine took over. "Allow me to make introductions. This is Jessica's friend and temporary roommate, Miss Becky Jo Osborne. Becky Jo, this is Captain Andrew Keegan."

"Pleased to meet you, Captain Keegan."

Drew stood and took the hand as it was offered, palm down, wrist slightly limp. He hadn't served time at Virginia cotillions without learning a little something. He bent again, from the waist, and lightly brushed a kiss on the soft skin of Becky Jo's very fragrant hand. He raised his head and stared into eyes the color of Texas bluebonnets.

"What a pleasure to meet you," he said sincerely, still holding her hand.

"The pleasure is all mine," Becky Jo responded sweetly.

A disgusted gag resonated from Jessica's direction as Frasier quietly chewed on the leather tie of Drew's shoe.

"Break it up, you two. I think we'd best scoot along before it gets much later," Valentine cautioned. "Drew wants to work out the finances this evening and it's getting on toward supper, so I think we'd better get a move on."

"Ladies." He inclined his head.

Jessica's smile was forced.

Becky Jo's was downright sappy.

Frasier growled.

Drew followed the women's eyes as they all looked down to see the dog pawing an open bag of potting soil, sending sprays of dirt in every direction. It was too late to jump out of the way. Soil cascaded across Drew's foot, clung to the slobbery lace and then fell neatly down between his fresh cotton sock and leather shoe.

He shook his foot in mild annoyance, stepped carefully around the mess, nodded goodbye and turned toward the exit.

"Talk to you dahhhlin' girls shortly," Valentine drawled just before the door closed behind her.

"Is that guy perfect for you, or what?" Becky Jo enthused as she herded Frasier back inside.

"You're as crazy as you look."

"Uh-uuuuh," was the singsong reply. "That big

man is class all the way and he's just what you need to get your mind off that Larry Bird wanna-be.''

Jessica held up her hands in surrender. The last thing she wanted to do was talk about the basketball forward who'd quietly dumped her several months earlier. He'd made some excuse about being too busy for a relationship. She knew the real reason he was suddenly so busy. What man would ever have time for an out-of-work, out-of-shape, overweight dancer?

A low rumble rattled the windows.

''What was that?'' Becky Jo gathered her caftan up around generous thighs and closed the distance to the laundry room.

''Check this out! Hurry!'' She frantically waved Jessica toward the window.

Urgency in her friend's voice caused Jessica to take the three steps up to the kitchen level with less caution than usual. Briefly aware there was no pain in the ascent, she silently thanked the hairy mutt whose needs forced her into motion every morning.

Standing on tiptoe, Becky Jo had pulled the mini-blinds several inches apart, revealing the commotion outside. Jessica had to stoop to peek through the same opening.

The temperature had been so nice all day that she'd opened several windows. The sound of a car engine carried through the screens, and it was loud! But it wasn't just noise.

Power reverberated.

Outside their laundry room was what guys lovingly

called "a muscle car." She didn't have to know anything about racing to know she was looking at a special machine. Painted a brilliant blue, the sports car had two wide white stripes across the top that ran the entire length of the vehicle. Extra-wide tires were mounted on shiny chrome wheels, pathetically clean compared to Jessica's grungy red station wagon.

The rumble grew as the car fell in behind Valentine's. The driver wore a harness instead of the usual seat belt. As if sensing female attention, Drew Keegan turned and gazed up at the window. Smiling in a way he probably knew deepened his dimples, he waved as if they were spectators in a private parade, revved the engine and passed through the gates of Sacred Arms.

The kitchen phone jangled. Jessica grabbed it on the second ring.

"Well, what do you think of Drew?" Valentine purred into her cell phone. "Isn't he a gorgeous creature?"

Jessica rolled her eyes. Valentine had never been subtle about her matchmaking. "He's okay, if you're into the macho military type, which I absolutely am not. As long as he keeps his distance, I'm sure we'll be just fine."

"Then you may have a small problem."

"Oh? Why is that?" Jessica asked, suddenly concerned at the humor lacing Valentine's voice.

"Dahhhlin', Captain Keegan is your new next-door neighbor."

Chapter Two

Just before 7:00 a.m., Jessica perched on the kitchen stool waiting for the first dose of caffeine of the day to drip. She yawned and gracefully stretched long arms overhead, flinching at the slight pain in her sunburned shoulders.

Frasier nudged at her ankle, demanding his morning walk. Ignoring his urgency would result in a puddle on the tile, so she took the leash from a peg by the front door.

"Come on, buddy. Let's head for the back lawn."

At the dog's insistence, she navigated the pathway a little more quickly each day. She preferred to start off slowly, letting her muscles warm up naturally. But there'd been little of that since Becky Jo had shown up on April Fool's Day with the critter under her arm. What an unexpected gift they'd been.

The accident had left Jessica lying on the couch for

months, burying her grief and guilt in bags of cookies. Unable to give up the practice of her daily weigh-in, she'd watched the number on the scale rise as she scoured childhood memories for the sin that had surely earned her body God's wrath.

Her only distraction was her lifelong best bud, who had kept the phone wires hot between Atlanta and Dallas. Becky Jo had been there day and night for Jessica to lean on, in the same way she leaned upon the detestable aluminum cane.

A month ago she'd answered the loud pounding on her front door to find the sweetest sight of her life— Rebecca Josephine Osborne standing in the hall with a squirming white dog firmly tucked in the crook of her arm. She'd come to stay awhile. Subletting her apartment to a college student, Becky Jo had packed up her eccentric retro wardrobe and folded her massage table into the back of her turquoise van.

Somewhere along the more than seven hundred miles of I-20, a tape had jammed in her eight-track player. Desperate for company, she'd located the animal shelter in the next small town and adopted Frasier. In a way peculiar to Becky Jo, she'd reasoned that a dog would be good physical therapy for her friend. Fortunately, she'd been right.

Every morning Becky Jo set off for the health spa and Jessica found herself the pup's primary caregiver. For the past month the rascal had kept her in constant motion. She stretched to move things out of his reach, bent to attach his leash and picked up the pace to keep up with his insistent tugging.

Frequent walks kept her mind off her problems and forced her to critically assess the beds and gardens she'd agreed to develop four years earlier when the property owner, Daniel Ellis, had reduced the price of her town home in exchange for her horticultural services.

Now, if she spotted a weed, it had to be pulled. Empty spaces in the perennial island had to be filled. As spring flowers bloomed, she became aware of the need for more balance, more texture or color. Folding new life into the soil was only surpassed by the satisfaction of admiring the results.

She was doing just that while she waited for Frasier to finish his morning business when a big dual-cab pickup pulled a rental trailer through the gates. The driver propped his elbow on the ledge of the open window, his muscular arm visible. He sported a baseball cap, his eyes hidden by dark sunglasses, but there was no mistaking that goofy little mustache or the very solid jaw.

Rambo.

Her stomach did a quick flip-flop.

Dropping her gaze self-consciously, she grimaced at the cheap shorts and tank top. Recent purchases, but already permanently stained. Her sneakers were old favorites, well past their prime. Even with one pinkie toe visible where the canvas had worn completely through, she refused to discard them.

She reached up, running a hand through the mess she called morning hair, and slid a disapproving tongue across fuzzy teeth. Worse still was the glow from fish-belly-white skin on exposed arms and legs. A little sunburn helped, but frying to a crisp wouldn't eliminate that fresh layer of cellulite that puckered just below the surface.

Anxiously she glanced up the path, seeking an escape route.

"Let's go, Frasier." She yanked the leash to get his cooperation. "Hurry up the front way, and we'll avoid him."

They made the long climb with the dog determined to stop every few feet. If Drew Keegan came around the corner for any reason, they'd be spotted. She could only hope he was completely occupied backing the trailer into place.

The pair made it to the Commons without incident. For once, Frasier chose to be quiet. A frisky squirrel could change that in a flash.

As they edged toward the corner, shoes crunched on the nearby pavement. Jerking the white pup to a halt, she held her breath and waited. Quick footsteps closed in. In a last-ditch effort at hair maintenance she ran jittery fingers through the tangles.

"Jessica, dahhhlin', good morning."

"Oh." Jessica dropped all pretense of feminine vanity. "It's only you, Valentine."

The older woman's face spread into a knowing

smile. "I see your handsome new neighbor just pulled up."

"Yes, and I'm glad it was just you who caught me like this."

Valentine regarded Jessica. "Now that you mention it, you're not exactly at your best."

"Well, it's early and you're the only woman I know who can look great at this hour of the morning."

Valentine patted her platinum hair lightly and smoothed the collar of a powder-blue silk jacket. "A girl must have her priorities straight." She lowered her voice discreetly. "You know, Captain Keegan is the son of Senator Marcus Keegan of Virginia."

"*The* Marcus Keegan? The guy who led the impeachment hearings?"

"One and the same."

"Okay, I can take a hint," Jessica conceded with a sigh. She glanced around nervously, hoping for a quick getaway.

Valentine noted her friend's agitation. "I've got an early appointment with a client, so I have to run. I just wanted to make sure Captain Keegan had the right security code."

Jessica gave a quick peck to the artfully made-up cheek. "See you later."

Resuming her purposeful walk, Valentine jingled her keys excitedly and set off to meet the client who would undoubtedly be signing a contract.

Jessica stood rooted to the same spot, unable to

decide which way to go. She gripped the blue leash tightly and peeked around the corner. The tall man bent from the waist and reached for something behind the seat of the truck. She seized her chance, punched in the security code and flung open the door. Balancing on her good leg, she jammed her cane in the opening so the door wouldn't close before she and the dog scooted inside.

Frasier stretched his tether to its fullest to investigate a beetle that had found its way into the marble vestibule.

"Come on, buddy," she whispered. "This is no time to get friendly with a stinkbug."

Another quick tug on the nylon cord and she had his full attention. He trotted forward. As she moved the cane, he suddenly dashed through the doorway at full speed. She released her grip, the only alternative to tumbling in after him. She turned in the direction of his excited barking, mortified.

It was him. Right there in the hallway. Not at the truck.

He stooped to greet her pet. Annoyance grew as the little mutt lavished the guy with kisses normally reserved for the person who filled the dog's supper bowl.

Drew smiled down the length of the corridor.

What could she do but pretend the entrance was timed perfectly? She squared her shoulders beneath yesterday's work shirt and turned her unwashed face straight in his direction. She made her way down the hall, leaning heavily on the cane to relieve the mild ache that generally accompanied the morning's walk.

"Moving day, huh?" she asked casually.

"Yes. I didn't think I'd get in this fast, but Ms. Chandler was great about pushing everything through for me."

Jessica nonchalantly folded her arms across her chest and leaned casually against the wall.

"Once Valentine makes up her mind she's found a good match for one of her properties, there's precious little that stands between her and a closing."

"She's an unusual woman, isn't she?" he asked.

"She's definitely in a class by herself."

"Um-hmm," he agreed with a smile.

Jessica's chest tingled at the sight of boyish dimples, and she dropped her eyes rather than return the smile. He was more casual today, dressed for the move in sneakers and creased denims. The neatly tucked racing T-shirt showed signs of having been properly folded right out of the dryer.

Their eyes met again. His kind smile threw her off balance. Literally. Her shoulder began to slide backward, down the wall. Her weight had been on her recovering leg and she didn't dare kick out with her other foot to counter the backward movement of her torso.

Instinctively both arms cast out, hands grasping at the air in front of her. With eyes squeezed shut, she waited for the pain sure to accompany a fall. Instead she felt an iron grip on her wrists, and then her face crushed against a rock-solid surface. Warm muscular arms enfolded her.

Drew had moved so quickly she hadn't heard a sound, just felt the security of being rescued. She held her breath, aware of a faint thumping, a light drumming. As she prepared to push away from the heartbeat and circle of protection, the security door creaked behind them.

"Well, I'm glad to know you're already getting a little Southern hospitality."

Jessica looked in the direction of the newcomer and then into the eyes of the man who held her in an awkward embrace.

She flushed with embarrassment.

Drew released her, but kept a secure grip on one arm as she leaned for her cane.

"Jessica, this is my business partner, Hank Delgado. Hank, this is my new neighbor, Jessica Holliday."

She offered the tall, silver-haired man what was surely a weak smile and ran a shaky hand through her hopeless mane.

"Hi, pleased to meet you." They shook hands over Frasier's excited effort to sniff up another stranger. "Your partner here just saved me from hitting the floor like a deflated volleyball." She nodded with gratitude at Drew as she spoke, silently vowing never to leave her front door again without makeup and clean clothes.

"If you gentlemen will excuse me, I think I'll see if my coffee is ready."

"Coffee sounds great. I take mine black." The older man spoke up.

"Well, sure." She turned to Drew. "And you?" she asked reluctantly.

What could she possibly do but be gracious after he'd literally caught her in his arms? Becky Jo would hoot over this.

"Nothing for either of us." Drew eyed his partner pointedly, acknowledging they hadn't been offered any coffee. "But thanks."

"Oh, go ahead and get us both a cup. I'll just haul another load of your stuff out of the truck. Take your time, son."

"I don't mind." She relented.

"If you're sure."

She smiled weakly and nodded.

"Thanks, Hank. I'll be right out. The front door's unlocked. Just sit boxes anywhere on the floor and I'll put them where they belong later."

"Nice to meet you, Jessica." Hank turned toward the exit, exposing a long, thin, rat-tail braid that fell about eight inches below his collar.

"You, too, Mr. Delgado."

"It's Hank," he called over his shoulder as he passed through the security door. "Mr. Delgado was my daddy."

Jessica pulled a key from her pocket. The lock turned easily. Frasier rushed ahead and up the stairs in search of some doggie treasure. The inviting aroma beckoned from behind the ficus grove. Leaning heavily upon the cane, she navigated the usual articles strewn about the floor. She turned behind the potted trees and climbed the steps to the kitchen landing.

Drew hesitated in the doorway hoping for a true invitation.

"Hello?" Her voice carried from the kitchen.

"Yes, I'm here."

"Well, why don't you come on up and help yourself? It's kind of hard for me to carry three cups these days."

That was the only request he was likely to get. He picked his way carefully through the maze of colorful throw pillows that had been tossed or dragged off the furniture. His fingers twitched to return the cushions to their rightful places.

"Cream and sugar?"

"Just sugar, please."

He rounded the greenery to get his first look at the kitchen, where a garden of potted ferns dangled from the ceiling. Her ceramic mug sat on the counter next to a stack of paper cups, the steaming brew waiting. Piles of magazines teetered on the ledge, pages dog-eared, notes jotted on a nearby legal pad.

Drew couldn't help but appraise the woman before him. If it were possible, she was even more rumpled than she had been at their first meeting. But something about her was so appealing.

Clear fair skin was creased with faint lines around

her wide-set eyes. There could be a crayon named for the unique shade of green, but he wasn't sure. He did, however, know lots of words to describe her mass of blond hair. He fought the desire to reach out and touch the soft tangles that danced around her shoulders.

Excited barking echoed from the loft upstairs.

"Would you excuse me for a minute? I need to see what that animal is up to." She edged past him.

"Sure." He hesitated for a moment and then added, "I must be intruding. I'll just fill our cups and be on my way."

"That's okay. My time is pretty much my own these days, so my work can wait. There's the sugar. Make yourself at home. I'll be right back."

She disappeared around the trees and he heard her steady climb up the stairs. Trained to note even the smallest detail, he let his eyes sweep the rest of the kitchen and dining area. There was clutter everywhere. Not trash, because everything seemed clean and useful. Just clutter. The kind he'd been taught to avoid or correct.

Gardening supplies filled every available space. The built-in wall unit, intended as a china hutch, instead displayed every conceivable hand tool for digging and planting. Judging from the seedling plants crowded onto the pine table and countertops, the local produce market was under serious threat. He sipped cautiously and studied the tags identifying the new crop as cucumbers and squash.

Jessica made her way back down the stairs. She'd changed into a faded T-shirt and pulled her thick sandy-blond hair into a neat ponytail. He smiled appreciation.

"If you like yellow squash, you've come to the right place."

He glanced around the room slowly, his gaze finally coming to rest on her incredible mossy eyes.

"It looks that way. Actually, I'm wondering how you find the space to cook and serve with all the gardening paraphernalia you've got in here."

"I don't do much of either," she confessed. "We mostly order in or go out for meals, or I just microwave something. For years I lived on poached fish and steamed vegetables. It's about the only thing I learned to cook, since it only required minimal effort."

"From what I've seen of your work so far, you don't seem like the kind of person who avoids effort."

"Oh, it's not that." She shook her head. "I've worked hard all my life to make things happen for myself."

He nodded understanding, remembering too well his own misguided concept of being the one in control.

"It's just that I never had the time to cook," she admitted. "When you're young and don't have plans for a family right away, you don't worry about learning things like that. When I finished college I went straight to work. Until a few months ago, there was never any time. So I didn't bother to learn.''

She hooked the handle of her cane over the high-backed kitchen chair and continued, ''My mama's a great cook. Maybe one day I'll practice some of the things I used to watch her do in the kitchen.''

Drew set his cup on the saucer as he wondered about her injury. ''Then we have something in common. My mother is...*was* a great cook, too.'' His mother had been lost years ago at the hands of a drunk driver, and he still had a hard time thinking of her in the past tense.

''Next time my sister sends me a box of her home-made Tollhouse cookies, I'll share them with you,'' he offered.

''My favorite! It's a deal.''

For the first time, she gave him a sincere smile. As it spread across her face, her eyes rose at the corners and crinkled around the edges. His breath caught in his throat when the eyes narrowed and flashed in good humor. His chest tingled in the strangest way.

He made a mental note to stick with the decaf he normally drank instead of indulging in this strong Southern brew.

''I'd better get back outside. As it is, Hank is going to give me a hard time about letting him do all that work by himself.''

''You said he's your partner?''

''Yeah. I'd known him for a couple of years buying parts over the phone from Metro Muscle. We finally met a few months ago at a car show. I've always liked this area, so I talked Hank into selling me part of his restoration business.''

''Good karma.'' Jessica's head bobbed up and down.

''I don't believe in karma, but I do believe Hank will put a knot on my head if I don't get back outside and finish unloading. We still have a full day of moving ahead of us.''

''If you need anything…''

''Actually, I was wondering about the churches in this area.''

''Sorry, that's not my strong suit. But if you're looking for an ice-cream shop—'' she patted her hip ''—I'm your resource.''

''I'll remember that.''

He picked up the two cups and backed away from the counter, not really wanting to break eye contact with this intriguing woman. He shifted his body, but not his face, toward the door. Finally, as he turned to make his exit, a cascade of ivy blocked his view and he smacked his head into a hanging basket.

He ducked just as the plastic bucket made a second sweep in his direction.

Jessica steadied the swinging plant. ''Did you hurt anything?''

''Only my pride,'' he admitted, rubbing his temple.

He stared into the enchanting face as her expression changed from concern to humor. Suddenly she burst into laughter. Throwing a hand over her mouth, she shook her head in apology.

"I'm sorry. You just looked so silly with that ivy draped over your head."

She followed him through the living room, unable to draw a breath without breaking into fresh giggles.

As he opened the door and stepped over the threshold, her infectious humor caught up with him. Just before he pulled the door closed behind him, he puckered his lips and blew her a noisy kiss.

Out in the hallway Drew stood still, appalled at the very personal gesture. The impulsive motion was completely out of character for a man who believed God had sent him on a mission to reconnect with a woman from his past.

During a brief college romance with Amelia Crockett, she'd proposed a deal.

When you get tired of playing army and want some real excitement, come find me in Atlanta. I'll be the perfect political partner for you.

A dozen years and a nearly fatal training mission later, he was prepared to take her up on the offer.

The heavy exterior door swung open. Hank carried an armload of clothing through the vestibule into the hallway. Several garments slid off the stack, falling into a soft heap on the floor.

"I've got it," Drew called, hurrying to close the space between them. He set the cups down carefully and then reached to recover his favorite wool suit, a starched dress shirt and two expensive cashmere sweaters. He brushed at the dark grains on the white shirt, but the motion only turned the small specks into streaks.

His nose twitched at the slight odor. Bending to the pristine broadcloth, he sniffed. Mingled with starch and laundry detergent was the unmistakable smell of…

Manure.

Chapter Three

Jessica was trapped, struggling for breath. She kicked frantically at the sheets that bound her in the semi-conscious state. Her groggy mind cast back to a room filled with skinny fifteen-year-old girls.

She stood out from them like a marshmallow in a bowl of pretzels, with thirty extra pounds on her body and a number forty-seven pinned to her back.

The instructor began leading the young dancers through combinations. Many struggled to keep up, but some caught on quickly. Jessica caught on. She fixed her attention on the movements, intent on copying and remembering them. When the pianist added music, the combinations became fluid, purposeful motions with a destination.

After the first hour a judge called out thirty numbers. These girls would continue the audition; the rest were free to go.

Number forty-seven made the cut.

The pace quickened as the instructor switched from basic ballet to moderately difficult jazz. It was obvious which dancers had the ability to cross over from classic to contemporary.

At the second break, fifteen more mothers packed up their daughters and headed for home. Jessica was grateful to be among the survivors, waiting for round three to begin.

The last part of the audition was modern dance, incorporating difficult leaps. The liability of her weight was evident in Jessica's landings.

Finally the audition ended and the girls were dismissed. There were only five scholarships available for the summer workshop. Ten losers would be spending the steamy days in small Texas towns, babysitting and watching MTV, while the winners worked with seasoned professionals.

Jessica swallowed the nervous lump in her throat and headed for the ladies' room. As she stood in line outside the door, she overheard the number forty-seven mentioned by a young, high-pitched voice. The discomfort reflected on the face of the girl directly in front of Jessica was no preparation for the blows that followed.

The shrill voice echoed inside the tiled walls. "What a country hog! I heard there were some big ones over in east Texas, but she's gotta be a blue ribbon winner."

Laughter followed the comment as another anonymous girl chimed in, "My mom says they have to let a few porky ones audition every year just so nobody can claim discrimination. If you ask me, it was just a waste of two good dance positions on the stage!"

The girls exited, laughing at their crude comments. Turning the corner, they came face-to-face with the butt of their jokes.

A very slender brunette gaped wide-eyed at Jessica. Embarrassed at being caught, the girl burst into nervous laughter and sprinted the distance to the auditorium. Jessica had heard the ugly words before, but they'd never penetrated in quite this way.

Inside the audition hall, the final results had been posted. Number forty-seven was not one of the scholarship winners, but neither were the numbers of the two from the rest room. Bittersweet, but small consolation.

Jessica bit a quivering lip and lifted her chin as a lone tear slipped down her cheek. Mama said God gave her a beautiful body and it was precious in His sight. But there was nothing precious about a girl called "porky."

Jessica jolted awake in a flushed panic, unable to shake the dream. It was always the same. And why not? It was more than a dream. It was a memory.

Nature had played a cruel trick, giving her a craving for sweets and a body that efficiently turned sugary comforts into lumpy cellulite. All the years of physical work and self-denial were for nothing. She was right back where she'd started.

The old digital clock clicked as the plastic numerals for 6:25 dropped into place. She tossed off the covers, pulled back the heavy drapes, cranked open two sets of louvered windows and slid back between wrinkled sheets.

At the foot of the bed, Frasier contentedly gnawed his sock monkey. She rolled across the king-size mattress to stroke his silky ears. The contact was reassuring.

Suddenly his head popped up. He appeared to listen for signs of activity outside the windows. He began to bark just as she picked up the strong downbeat. She struggled to her feet while Bruce Springsteen informed the world he was born in the U.S.A.

A glance at the parking lot below gave no clue as to the music's origin, but it was so close. And so loud. It seemed to come…right through the wall.

"Rambo! I knew it! I knew that guy was going to be trouble."

She yanked on the flowered chenille robe Becky Jo had bought at a thrift store for seventy-five cents.

With a firm grip on her cane and Frasier hot on her heels, she took the stairs in record time, flung open her front door and closed the space between the two homes. As she drew back to pound on the door, it opened, placing her face-to-face with silver-haired Hank Delgado.

Frasier scooted past the long legs and slid across

the polished wood floor. He made a muffled "umph" sound as he nose-dived into a leather ottoman.

"Good morning." Hank cocked an eyebrow at Jessica as if he wondered what she looked like with her hair combed.

"It was, until somebody gave the order to crank it up."

"The boy gets up at the crack of dawn, and he does like his music loud." He nodded agreement, pressing hands against his ears in an exaggerated fashion.

She tried her best to seem angry. It didn't work. She dropped her head to hide the smile that threatened. Acutely aware of her bare feet, she imagined how foolish she must appear, standing in the hallway in the ancient robe.

"My mama had a housecoat just like that. I think she donated it to the thrift store over on Peachtree," he said with a reminiscent smile.

Jessica didn't even want to consider the possibility.

"Hey, man, it's the welcoming committee," Hank shouted to his partner.

Drew glanced over his shoulder and his eyes widened in surprise. He gave Jessica's robe a nod and a cheerful thumbs-up.

So much for yesterday's vow never to leave the house again without clean clothes and makeup. She realized that for the third time this guy had caught her at her worst. Of course, he was spit shined and polished already. It wasn't fair for a man to look so well put together this early in the morning.

"I know I said I'd have you over, but I thought you'd at least give me a day to unpack," Drew called.

Hank reached for the stereo to turn down the volume.

Drew moved into the doorway to greet his visitor. "Well, don't just stand there." He motioned with his hand. "Come on in."

She stepped into his home for the first time, admiring the deep muted tones of the rugs and furnishings, the rich smell of new leather and the bookcase filled with handsome volumes. A worn Bible lay atop the sofa table.

"Did you really move in less than twenty-four hours ago?" She noted how few boxes remained unpacked.

"I believe in a place for everything and everything in its place." Drew smiled with pride. "Hey, I just happen to have a fresh pot of Colombian decaf." He stared pointedly at Jessica's bare feet. "But isn't it a little early for you to be paying a social call?"

"Isn't it a little early for you to be playing your stereo so loud?"

"You don't like the Boss? I suppose you'd prefer something different?"

"As a matter of fact, Springsteen is one of my all-time favorites. But at this hour of the morning, I do like my music a little more soothing."

"For instance?" he asked, stooping to inspect his considerable collection of compact discs.

"Well, for instance…" She groped for something to catch him off guard. "Rachmaninoff appeals to me in the mornings."

"Is that right?" he asked in a "gotcha" tone.

Selecting a CD from one of several towers, he dropped it into a multidisc player. Within moments the room swelled with the sound of a single keyboard accompanied by a section of violins. He reached to increase the volume, stopping short, hand just above the control.

She'd never have admitted it at that moment, but he'd impressed her.

"You like *classical* music?" she questioned with disbelief.

"Music lessons were not optional at my house. My sister and I had to choose an instrument in the sixth grade and stick with it through graduation. I chose the piano."

"Because of all the great composers?"

"No. Because I figured since it was too big to carry around with me, I could keep the guys at school from finding out about it. I don't think I've ever said that out loud before."

"I promise not to tell your dark secret, as long as you promise to watch the decibel level of your stereo." She fixed him with an accusing stare. "At least before nine o'clock in the morning."

Drew ducked his chin, appropriately contrite. "Sorry. I didn't realize it was so loud."

"The heck, you say!" Hank stepped down from the kitchen. "I told you it was gonna wake somebody up, but you were too busy singing along to care." Hank turned to her. "You ought to hear how loud he has Jimmy Buffett blasting through the showroom down at Metro."

Drew's eyes widened. "All you had to do was say something."

Hank gestured toward the stereo. "But that stuff right there is kinda nice. Why don't you bring that CD down to the shop with you tomorrow?"

"Well, I'll just have to do that."

She glanced from one man to the other, thinking what an odd but colorful team they made, the fifty-something laid back and the thirtysomething uptight.

Hank offered his mug in salute. "Jessica, I owe you one. Come on down to Metro Muscle and I'll make you a good deal on an old car."

"Thanks, but I already have an old car."

"If you change your mind…" He smiled and headed back to the kitchen.

She turned to leave.

Stepping between his guest and the door, Drew reached for the knob and then paused.

"By any chance would your old car be that rusty station wagon with all the gardening supplies stacked next to it?"

Her trouble sensors went on full alert. She was torn

between pride in the beloved vehicle and suspicion for why he was asking. But she answered honestly.

"That's my Ruby."

"Ruby?"

"Sure, that's her name. Ruby Red."

He squinted, confusion etched on his face.

"You seem to care a lot about automobiles. I bet that blue car has a name," she said matter-of-factly.

Drew glanced over her head toward his partner. Jessica followed his gaze to see Hank busy with the installation of the clothes dryer. Her neighbor looked back at her, leaning in closer.

"Okay. Normally when I tell this to someone, I have to kill them. But I think I can trust you." He lowered his voice. "When we're alone, just me and the hot rod, I call him…" He glanced toward the laundry room again and whispered, "Rambo."

She gasped, first embarrassed, then angry. The big goon burst into loud laughter. She made a fist and gave a solid punch to his shoulder. His face registered surprise at the strength of the blow. He winced and rubbed the spot, but continued to enjoy his laugh at her expense.

"Who told you?" She demanded an answer.

"You mean more than one person knows about my nickname?"

She couldn't help noticing when he laughed that there were twin dimples in his tanned cheeks. It only made him more attractive.

"Well, I guess I have called you that a time or

two...." She held up a hand in defense as his eyes opened wide in mock surprise. "But you have to admit, it's an obvious comparison under the circumstances."

"And what exactly are the circumstances?" He arched a dark eyebrow in challenge.

Realizing no good could come from continuing the conversation, she opened the door and prepared to leave. Drew moved toward her and she blocked any advancement with the end of her cane aimed squarely at his broad chest. The image of a lion tamer using a chair to hold off the king of beasts came to her mind.

"Okay," he conceded. "You're not the first person to typecast me in that role. But do me a favor and get to know me a little better before you label me. Fair enough?"

She slowly lowered the cane back to its usual place, beside her right leg.

"Fair enough."

Jessica caught sight of her dog, watching from atop a leather recliner. "Come on, Frasier, let's go home."

His head cocked to the left when he heard his name, but he stayed in his comfortable position. She snapped her fingers and pointed to the floor beside her heel. Frasier dropped his chin and closed his eyes. She heaved an exasperated sigh.

"Before you go, I need to ask—where do you plan to store all those bags of fertilizer you have stacked beside your car?"

"I hadn't really given it much thought. Why? Are they in your way?"

"Let's just say I'd enjoy the view a great deal more if they weren't cluttering up the parking lot."

"Then let's also say you wouldn't be enjoying the view at all if I didn't have easy access to the bags when I need them." She stepped outside the door into the hallway.

He tried a smaller request.

"I expect you'll at least sweep the walk and the hallway clean after you finish for the day."

Jessica took her weight off the walking stick and straightened to her full height. Standing taller than most women could, and probably closer than most men dared, she fixed him with an icy stare. "What branch of the service did you say you were in again?"

"The United States Army, Special Forces." He stared right back.

"What was your title?"

"*Is*. My rank *is* Captain."

"Well, *Captain* Keegan of the United States Army, Special Forces, I am not one of your new hires, or recruits, or privates, or whatever you call them, so don't presume to talk to me like one. I am the woman who lives next door. Your neighbor. I'll do my best to clean up any mess I make. You do your best to hold the noise down and we'll get along fine."

She looked from the bemused hazel eyes over to the ones that peeked through a veil of white hair.

Snapping her fingers and pointing beside her foot, she said in a calm but firm voice, "Frasier. Heel!"

With no hesitation, the dog jumped to the floor.

Drew watched as the pup followed the bare feet beneath the colorful robe back to their own door, where it closed firmly behind them both.

"I'd say you handled that pretty well." Hank leaned against the bookcase, shaking his head.

"What'd I say wrong?" Drew asked, completely confused.

"Didn't your mama teach you that you catch flies with honey, not vinegar?"

"I suppose you would have handled it differently?"

"Son, you need some coaching. For such a smart kid, you are completely lacking any female emotion sensors." Hank made himself at home on the sofa, crossing one worn-out boot over the other, then continued.

"Well, the way I see it, you've got two choices. You can make friends with that woman, help her see things your way, or you can knock heads with her and not accomplish a blasted thing. You've been here twenty-four hours and she's mad at you already. If you don't make some effort to change that soon, it's only gonna get worse."

While Drew considered his friend's comment, he absentmindedly straightened a pillow askew from the dog's visit. One of his primary reasons for being in

Atlanta was a woman. He was going to have his hands full when he started that project. The last thing he needed was a difficult female next door.

"Okay, what do you suggest?"

"Think of this as a military situation. You need to turn an enemy into an ally. What's your strategy?"

Finally on familiar ground, Drew took heart. He perched on the edge of an ottoman considered oversize for most. For him, it was a perfect fit.

"First I evaluate the opponent's position. What are his strengths and weaknesses? What does he stand to gain or lose from an alliance? How can we mutually benefit from me helping him reach his own goals?"

"That's a beginning," Hank drawled. "Now start thinking in terms of *her* instead of him and start calling her your neighbor instead of your opponent."

"Got it." Drew made a mental check mark.

"So, what do you see as her strengths?"

Hank leaned back, threading long fingers behind his head.

"She's a beautiful woman with a strong right cross." Drew massaged the shoulder where she'd punched him. "She's obviously blessed with a green thumb, seems to be very honest and she's certainly not afraid to speak her mind."

"You admire all those qualities, don't you?" Hank asked.

Drew had to think about that for a moment. He did admire them. Maybe that helped explain his strange behavior yesterday. He still struggled with the impulsively blown kiss.

"Yes, I do," he admitted.

"Now we're making progress. So what do you see as her weaknesses?"

This one would be even easier.

"She's a train wreck! You should see the inside of her home. It's a mess, too. I don't know how anybody can accomplish so much with poor organizational skills."

"This is starting to sound like a radio psychology show," Hank admitted. "But since you recognize her accomplishments, how do you suppose you could help her improve in the organization area?"

"I could go over there and offer her some pointers on how to get her house and her business in order." Drew thought it was a sensible idea.

"Yeah, you could do that. And I think she'd probably appreciate it like a roach in her potato salad."

"Too straightforward, huh?"

Both men nodded agreement.

Resting his elbows on the extra-wide leather chair, Drew leaned back to gaze at the vaulted ceiling. He'd always been the hardheaded, show-me type. Maybe Jessica was, too.

"Hank, have I ever told you the order and organization of Metro was the first thing about the business that won me over?" Drew complimented his new partner.

"At least a hundred times."

''Well, it was. That's important to me.''

''Obviously.''

''What if I invite Jessica to visit our shop and explain to her how great a place of her own could be?'' Drew asked.

Hank rolled his eyes.

''You're right, no female emotion sensors at all. I'll have to think of something else to get her down there.''

''How about that new place where they sell landscaping rock by the truckload?'' Hank offered. ''It just opened down the road from us and she may not even know about it yet.''

Drew's eyes narrowed as a plan took shape in his mind. He was nothing if not an expert at conceiving and following a plan. He'd honed his skills at West Point and completely embraced the love of organization in the Special Forces.

Hank looked up suspiciously. ''What are you up to, buddy? I've only seen that spark in your eyes once before and the next thing I knew you owned half my shop.''

Chapter Four

Jessica stood in the doorway of her walk-in closet, hoping an outfit she'd overlooked would magically catch her eye. It wasn't going to happen. She kept standing there, unable to accept defeat.

It wasn't too late to make a mad dash to the mall. But she'd be darned if she'd treat her neighbor's request for back-road guidance as a date, no matter how appealing he'd tried to make it sound.

He'd apologized for being pushy. He'd offered to make it up to her by showing her the new landscaping center in Jonesboro.

What a load of baloney. She suspected what she really wanted was somebody to show him the short-cuts between Sacred Arms and that Metro place so he could shave five minutes off his commute.

If he had a fuel-efficient vehicle like hers, instead of a gas-guzzling hot rod or monster truck, he wouldn't have to worry about a few extra miles a week. She shrugged to herself. What else would you expect from a testosterone-saturated creature who probably bought underwear in a package of six for ten dollars?

The door slammed and Frasier's manic barking heralded Becky Jo's arrival. The fashion consultant was here at last. Jessica tossed the only two possible options on her bed.

"Jessica?" Becky Jo called from the foot of the stairs.

"Up here, Beej. I'm having a crisis and I need your special brand of advice."

"Be right there," she yelled back. "Let me stop off in the kitchen for a soda."

Jessica surveyed the pitiful selections. One pair of jeans, size fourteen and miserably tight, lay on the bed like a virgin sacrifice. Steadfastly refusing to buy anything larger, she struggled into them on rare occasions, hiding the bulge at her waist with a shirt worn untucked. Probably the oldest fat trick in the book, but the only one she knew.

Second choice was a relatively new pair of khaki walking shorts. She'd spent so much time outdoors lately that her legs had a little color. When she sat down, her thighs spread out to twice their size. If she put her weight on her toes and pressed upward, it lifted her legs off the seat and that helped some. But she'd never make it all the way to Jonesboro like that without getting a cramp.

Dressing was a no-win situation. She'd go next door, say "no, thanks" and offer to draw him a map.

Becky Jo made her entrance. She drank deeply from a crystal goblet, sighed dramatically and affected an exaggerated swoon onto the bed, never spilling a drop. She admired her own abundant form and new gold lamé hostess pajamas.

Frequent trips to the thrift shop paid off, but yesterday she'd hit the jackpot. The new supply of plus-size silks and satins clearly indicated some rich society hostess had either lost weight or been shopping. Either way, Becky Jo was the beneficiary.

"Okay, what's the occasion, and who do we want to impress?" She cast a disapproving scowl at the jeans and shorts. "Please tell me I've got more to work with than this."

Jessica slumped to the bed and raked the clothes onto the floor. Her friend was right. Compared to the fashionable, bare midriff combinations she'd worn a year ago, these clothes were matronly.

"Our new neighbor asked me to ride down to Jonesboro with him tomorrow. He wants to learn the country roads, so he offered to show me a new garden supply near that garage of his."

Becky Jo sat up. "A date, huh?"

"No, it's not a date. Stop looking at me that way. I haven't had a date in months and I'm not likely to have one any time soon."

When Becky Jo pressed her lips together and

squinted, Jessica knew her lack of self-confidence was showing again.

"You'd be amazed how many men would like to take you out, if you'd just give them the chance," Becky Jo insisted.

"Yeah, right." Jessica's self-pity simmered just below the surface.

Becky Jo wiggled her index finger at Jessica. "You're thinking 'What nice-looking guy would be interested in a fat woman?' Aren't you?"

Jessica gasped at her best friend's bluntness. "I was not, and I never think of you that way."

Becky Jo's smile was sympathetic. "I know, Jess. I don't think of me as fat, either. Neither do the men I date. That's because I'm voluptuous and Rubenesque and bountiful and all the other great superlatives they use in fashion magazines to describe women of substance."

She stood and preened before the mirror, smiling in self-appreciation. "Plenty of men out there aren't set on a relationship with a scarecrow. Jess, if you'd lighten up a little bit, you'd find out for yourself."

Becky Jo's blue eyes brightened. "I've been waiting for just the right time to give you something. You dig out the sexiest tank top you have. I'll be right back."

Jessica began to pull spaghetti-strap tanks from her armoire. Finding a personal favorite, she fingered the butter-colored cotton and hand-tatted lace.

"Oh, that's perfect! Put it on." Becky Jo was back

with something made of stonewashed denim slung over one shoulder.

"It's too small now."

"Baloney! Will you stop whining about what's wrong with you and start taking advantage of what's right? For the first time in your life you have a chest that will stop traffic. Enjoy it."

Jessica had to agree with her friend. During her years of food deprivation there'd never been much up top. This fullness was new to her, too.

She'd changed costumes in theater wings a thousand times. Bodies weren't important then. Only talent seemed to matter. Now, self-conscious even with her dearest friend, she turned her back. Pulling the T-shirt over her head, she replaced it with the delicate lace garment that was hardly more than a camisole.

"As long as you're being shy, stay there and put this on. I picked them up for you at a garage sale."

Pale blue denim landed at Jessica's feet. She stepped out of worn work shorts into stretch cotton overalls. After the straps were fastened, only a hint of yellow lace showed above the bib and beneath her arms.

The pants were a bit too short. Before she could object, Becky Jo sat on the floor, cross-legged, and rolled the cuffs fashionably to just below the knee.

"I've always secretly hated you for tanning so well in the summer," she griped.

"Secretly?" Jessica laughed. "I've heard that from you every year since we were nine."

"Okay, so it wasn't a secret. Turn around and see how great these colors look on you, Jess."

How long had it been since she'd really noticed the full-length cheval mirror? Gazing at her reflection, Jessica couldn't disagree with the results.

"Wear your hair down for a change. Your blue sandals are perfect. I have some nail polish that will look fabulous! After dinner I'll do your toenails, but you have to do mine, too. What are we having for dinner, anyway?"

Becky Jo was gone, the last words trailing down the stairs. End of discussion. The fashion crisis had passed.

Jessica had a date.

The doorbell chimed the next morning, followed by the usual excited barking and then an abnormal silence. Halfway down the stairs, Jessica noticed that Frasier calmly sat at attention, patiently waiting for whoever was beyond the door.

She took her time. No need to appear anxious. As she reached the foyer, two more rapid chimes caused her to jump.

"All right! I heard you the first time!" She yanked open the door.

The surprise in Drew's eyes turned the sugary breath mint in her mouth to a sour ball.

He just stood there staring at her.

"What?"

"Excuse me, miss. I'm looking for my neighbor.

A lady about your height, stained clothes, ponytail, no makeup. Have you seen her around here anywhere?''

''Very funny.'' Stepping aside, she inclined her head as an invitation to enter.

Before crossing the threshold, he squatted to a catcher's position and offered the patient Frasier a peanut candy. The dog carried the treat behind the couch, where he munched it loudly.

''How'd you get him to sit still like that?''

''I gave him a command through the door. He's obviously been trained.'' He paused, eyes challenging. ''He's just not sure who's in charge.''

She glared right back. ''We'll have to work on that.''

Assuming they'd take his big truck, Jessica was pleasantly surprised when he proudly escorted her to his car. When she reached for the handle, he hurried to open her door. She slid into the seat, her cane across her lap.

Knowing next to nothing about racing, even she recognized the importance of cables that locked the hood in place and a fire extinguisher mounted in the back. He knelt and showed her how to secure the elaborate harness.

''Are you going to drive it or fly it?'' she asked nervously.

''That's really up to you.'' His mustache twitched above a small smile.

The old engine roared even louder from inside the

car. Wind whipped hair into her face, making conversation almost impossible. She said little, pointing directions and gesturing at mile markers along the way. They rode in silence, if you could call it that, for the first ten miles.

At her loud instruction, he took the Tara Boulevard exit and downshifted as they fed into the slower traffic. The car seemed to struggle physically against being restrained. Jessica regarded Drew to see if she imagined the sensation.

"You feel it, don't you?" He seemed pleased.

"Yes! Rambo wants back on the interstate."

They both laughed at the not-so-private joke.

"Tell me about yourself, Jessica."

"Why should I?" she teased.

"My family still lives in the same house where I grew up, so I've known our neighbors all my life," he began. "I'd like to know the residents at Sacred Arms, too. This seems like a good time to get started. Do you mind?"

"No, it's just been a while since anybody was interested in my life story. Where would you like me to start?"

"How about telling me how you got into gardening?"

She smiled at the memory.

"I think I was genetically predisposed to grow things. Mom always had a vegetable garden because money was so tight. It was just the two of us, so I helped out a lot. We planted flowers in the same beds with the vegetables to help keep the bugs away. I guess I picked up her love for it.''

''So you always wanted to do landscaping?''

''Not exactly. We decided it was a good backup to my dance career. As it turned out, it was a smart decision.''

''Dance career?'' he asked.

''Didn't Valentine tell you?'' Jessica was amazed her cagey friend had left some mystery for him to discover on his own.

''Ms. Chandler has more inside information than CNN, but she never mentioned anything about you and dancing. I'd remember.''

The last was said so sincerely that Jessica was encouraged to reminisce.

''For the past four years I was with the Atlanta Dance Theater.''

''Are you serious?'' He glanced away from the road to read her expression.

''I know it's kind of hard to believe, looking at me now.'' And because he was, she casually drew her feet closer to the seat and balanced on her toes. Thinking her thighs looked a little thinner, she met his eyes and continued. ''That was six months and about sixty pounds ago, before the car accident that tore up my knee.''

Considerately he ignored the reference to her weight. ''I wondered about your injury. I went through some serious recovery myself a while back. I know how devastating it can be to your life.''

"What kind of recovery?" She stared at him. He was the picture of robust health. This man couldn't possibly know how it felt to be broken, in body or spirit.

"Not so fast. We were talking about you. I want to hear more about this dance career."

"You really want to know?"

"I really want to know."

So she told him.

Drew smiled warmly at the image she spun of the little girl who loved to dance. Her voice held unmistakable pride when she told him about the college production of *Cats* that won her an audition with a cruise line's entertainment director.

"How long did that last?"

"Almost two years. It was great fun and there was a lot of creative freedom. But after a while the repetitiveness of the cruise routine got old. I wanted the challenge of a professional company and the chance to sink roots somewhere for a while."

She pointed to a rural route sign as she spoke and Drew made the sharp turn onto a small shaded road. There was no traffic, so he let the machine roar back to life for a couple of minutes.

She watched the muscles work in his right arm as he shifted smoothly through the five gears. Pretending to admire the restoration of the polished chrome console, she allowed herself to appreciate the contrast of his tanned arm against a navy polo shirt. She noted the fine layer of smooth dark hair that ended at his wrist and then reappeared lightly atop his fingers. His neatly trimmed nails were immaculate.

"So how'd you end up in Atlanta?"

The question startled her almost as much as the stirring she began to feel at admiring his very masculine arm.

"What?" She caught him grinning at her.

"I said how did you end up in Atlanta?"

"A-A-Atlanta?" She stammered the word, busted over a biceps. "Well, I wanted to stay in the South to be near my mom."

"Sounds like you two are very close."

"My father, who's ex-military by the way, left us when I was nine. He never helped with the bills or showed up when he said he would. Family life just wasn't his thing, and the more he let me down, the more my mom stepped up. So yeah, we're very close."

"Please don't blame your father's behavior on the military. There are men who have trouble settling down afterward, but we're not all like that."

"That's what everybody tries to tell me."

Drew motioned for her to continue.

"Anyway," she went on, "I started flying to auditions every time we docked for maintenance in Miami. When the ADT offered me a contract, I jumped at it."

"What about New York? Broadway? I thought that was every dancer's dream."

"Maybe for some. But living there never appealed

to me. I love visiting, but after a few days I'm ready to get out of that sea of people. Besides, I'm a Southern girl through and through. Mild winters and friendly strangers, you know?''

''I sure do. I've seen some of the biggest cities in the world, but none were places I wanted to call home. I'm thankful the good Lord gave me this opportunity to move back to Georgia.''

''You lived here before? I thought you and your family had always been in Virginia. After all, your dad is *the* Marcus Keegan, right?'' She was almost reluctant to mention the famous name, since Drew hadn't so far.

''The one and only,'' he said with admiration. ''I grew up in Great Falls, and my sister, Faith, still lives there with my dad.''

''So when were you in Georgia?''

''I was stationed at Fort Benning during Ranger school. After nine of the toughest weeks of my life, I spent some R and R at a buddy's home in Blue Ridge. It was a beautiful drive up from the base into the mountains. Another time I traveled a few hours into Florida and discovered one of the cleanest beaches in the world. That's when I decided that if the choice of settling down ever became mine, Georgia would be high on the list of favorite spots.''

''What do you mean, if the choice were yours?'' She studied the rugged profile accented by the trim mustache. She willed her hand not to reach across to touch the perfectly trimmed line of dark whiskers.

"I've been committed to a military career for as long as I can remember. When I made that commitment, I agreed to go wherever they sent me for as long as I was needed, no questions asked."

She struggled to imagine devotion of that magnitude. Certainly something her father hadn't possessed. Dance required discipline and dedication, but those things were born out of love for the art. It couldn't compare to what he'd been through.

"Did you always know you wanted to be a soldier?"

"I never got the chance to know what I wanted." He laughed to himself, but there was little humor in his voice when he spoke. "I always knew what my country and my father wanted. And now I know what God wants of me, so I'm focused on that."

"And what about what *you* want?"

Drew's somber eyes met Jessica's. "What *I* want has never been at the top of the list," he confessed. "As a soldier, God, country and family were my priorities. I think that's true for most servicemen. But it took me a long time to learn the value of truly putting God first on that list."

"Maybe those things were important to you, but never to my father," she scoffed.

Drew must have sensed her discomfort over the subject. When they both spied the marquee of the local ice-cream shop, he raised his eyebrows and inclined his head in invitation. A brief detour might be a nice way to break this serious spell. Pulling into the

Chapter Five

The temptation of sizzling burgers and crisp Vidalia onion rings beckoned Jessica from the drive-through window.

"You ready for some lunch?" Drew reached for his wallet.

"It's still a little early and I had a big breakfast," she lied, her sense of smell miserably tantalized. She'd love to indulge, but had promised herself a healthy diet for once. "But I will take that dipped cone you offered." Calcium would be good for a mending knee, she rationalized.

Two of the chocolate-coated temptations were passed through the window along with a stack of napkins. He handed her both cones and steered to a deserted spot on the far side of the parking lot. A carload of teenage boys pulled alongside his car almost immediately.

"Hey, mister, mind if we take a look under the hood?" Three young men climbed out of a parent's sensible sedan and headed their way.

Drew's door was already open, one clean sneaker crunching the gravel. "I'll just be a minute," he called.

"Are you serious? What about your ice cream?" she shouted through the window.

He reached down to release the hood. "Hold it for me, please. This won't take long."

At least, that's what she thought he said. The four heads were already buried behind the raised hood, a wall of brilliant blue and wide white stripes blocking her view. She heard a young male voice crack as he exclaimed over whatever they found so fascinating.

Dribbling ice cream, creeping down her fingers, demanded her full attention. A warm breeze stirred the air inside the car, hastening the melting process. With nowhere to set one cone while she cleaned up, the only option was to eat. And eat fast! Jessica alternately worked the edges of both cones. There was no time to worry about sanitary issues.

Twisting and twirling, she lapped up the melting ice cream that oozed beneath the thin crust of chocolate. Unable to resist, she bit the swirled tip from one of the glistening crowns and sucked a fragment into her mouth. Bad move. The fragile shell began to break apart and threatened to drop into her lap. The lap that was, for once, clean.

With a cry of dismay she struggled to consume the

avalanche of chocolate. A muscular arm shot through the window to relieve her of the second cone, freeing her hand for damage control.

Youths abruptly dismissed, Drew once again sat next to her, evidently amazed by her ability to attract stains to her clothing. She continued to struggle with her disintegrating dessert as tiny bits of chocolate fell and melted on her secondhand denim overalls. If it hadn't been so absurd, she'd have cried over the picture she surely made.

So much for her "date."

Quickly depositing his own mutilated treat into a handy disposal bag in the back seat, Drew grabbed a handful of napkins and turned to assist.

"Here, let me," he offered.

She sat like a helpless child, both hands a sticky mess, as he worked his way from her elbows to her chin. The immediate catastrophe under control, he slowed his pace. Their eyes met. Without hesitation, both burst into wide smiles that quickly became uncontrollable laughter.

Since she didn't dare touch her own face with gooey hands, tears of mirth streamed unchecked down her cheeks.

Unexpectedly he gently dabbed at them with a fresh napkin.

Jessica sobered. Her smile faded. She couldn't recall ever being touched by a man with such kind intent.

Drew quieted, too. His smile relaxed, but his eyes remained intense.

She felt the need to say something. "You didn't get any ice cream."

"It's not too late," he said softly as he bent his head toward hers, stopping just before their lips met.

She held her breath. He was so close. Her eyelids drooped in anticipation of what would surely be a kiss. She was afraid to breathe. Afraid to move. Afraid to open her eyes again for fear she'd been mistaken.

Then there was the smallest tickling sensation at the corner of her mouth. She remained still, transfixed, barely exhaling. Hot breath mingled with her own as he tasted the dried sugar on her lips. Not touching anywhere but their mouths, the two melted into one another.

"Hey, Drew, thanks a lot," the young driver of the sedan shouted. "We'll check your Web site."

The kiss interrupted, Drew waved away the boys without glancing their way. Her heart danced against her ribs as his chestnut gaze wandered over her face.

"I think there's only one way to finish what I've started," he said as he reached into his back pocket and fished out a small foil packet.

Jessica's eyes widened in shock, horrified that this man would arrogantly misread an innocent kiss!

She prepared to give him the sticky slap of his life when he turned and offered it to her.

"Wet nap?" he asked innocently.

"What?" She couldn't have heard him correctly.

"Do you want a wet nap to clean your hands? I always carry one with me," he offered.

"Somehow that doesn't surprise me," she snapped.

Metro Muscle sat on four acres of land in Jonesboro, not too far from where Margaret Mitchell had imagined Tara, the fabled home of Scarlett O'Hara. Whether a client's collectible was a classic sixties pony car or a brand-new model, Metro carried the reputation as the only place for connoisseur repair.

Drew pulled through the security gate and parked up front. Jessica had hardly spoken a word since she'd snatched the towelette from his hand and used it to scrub her hands and face clean. She'd made such a production of using it around her mouth that he was beginning to think she'd wanted to clean away his kiss.

Before he could open her door, she'd unfastened the harness and struggled to her feet. Even relying on her cane, she almost beat him to the front entrance.

The kiss had proved to be an error in judgment, because he was definitely in the doghouse. Throughout his career he'd excelled at analyzing opponents. But then, they'd always been rational thinking men.

As he admired the graceful curve of her figure, he was almost grateful this opponent was most definitely different.

Jessica stepped through the front door and into the sales area. She'd expected a garage filled with greasy parts and broken-down cars, never imagining the mirrored, carpeted showroom. In this place a man could recapture the first automotive love of his youth and a woman could understand why he'd want to.

A convertible beckoned her closer. Red! And magnificently restored.

"She's a beauty, isn't she? A '68 model." Drew's face reflected her appreciation of the car.

Forgetting her earlier agitation, she smiled as she ran her hand across the polished trunk. As she stepped forward to investigate the interior, she noticed he nonchalantly whipped a soft bandanna out of his hip pocket. He wiped the finish, removing all traces of her touch.

"In case you don't remember, I recently sanitized my hands," she reminded him.

"Don't take offense. Plenty of new clients don't know it's not cool to touch the paint. That's why we have the signs." He gestured to the framed poster by the door. The same message, Please Don't Touch, was displayed on a windshield placard.

"What's the big deal?" She couldn't imagine taking such care, even with her beloved Ruby. But, she had to admit, her lack of care was obvious.

"These are concours cars. Meaning everything used in the restoration process is original right down to the last wing nut. Accomplishing that with a thirty-year-old vehicle requires a lot of hard work and money. Owners allow very limited contact with their vehicles.''

''You mean I can't touch it?''

He swept open the door and removed the placard. ''You, Miss Holliday, may touch to your heart's content.''

She rolled her eyes and eased herself behind the wheel. ''I love the white interior,'' she enthused, running her hand over the upholstered leather seat.

''Parchment,'' he corrected. ''The color is called parchment.''

She imagined herself racing toward Savannah for the weekend, hair flying, sun shining. She dismissed the brief, impossible vision and reached for her cane.

More quickly this time, Drew was at her side offering his hand for support, which she accepted.

''Ready to see the back?''

''Sure,'' she agreed, no longer expecting just another greasy garage.

Drew passed through a heavy metal door and considerately held it aside. Her mild interest turned to full-blown respect. The walls were lined with floor-to-ceiling racks, filled with ancient parts. Everything from floor mats to fuel tanks appeared to be cleaned and categorized.

She moved among the shelves, realizing the time and patience it must have taken to inventory so many items. Glancing toward the repair bays, she was impressed with the organization of materials and equipment. The painted concrete floor was swept clean and a pressure washer stood at the ready.

"I never imagined a garage could be so tidy." She gave the devil his due.

Drew's already broad chest swelled at the compliment.

"Well, you know I believe in a place for everything and—"

"Everything in its place." She finished the platitude. "Yeah, you told me. Now I see why you leave early and come home late."

His head cocked slightly to the side. "You've noticed, huh?"

"That diesel truck engine is pretty hard to ignore before daylight. It's either you or a lost 18-wheeler." She arched a blond eyebrow.

They'd wandered back into the showroom. Drew produced a handful of change and dropped it into the soda machine. He stepped aside to let Jessica make a selection.

She popped the top on her diet soda and enjoyed a long drink.

"Well, what do you think?"

"I think it's all very impressive." She took another sip.

"It's too bad you don't make such a good first impression," he said.

Stunned by the insult, she inhaled some of the drink and began to choke, spewing cola atop the bits of melted chocolate on her overall bib. In an instant he was behind her, lifting her arms high over her head to help clear her windpipe.

Finally able to breathe, she pulled her arms free and rammed an elbow into the hard abdomen pressed to her back. It didn't have quite the painful impact she'd intended, but she was gifted with a small "whoosh" as Drew exhaled involuntarily.

"What was that for?" He rubbed his middle.

"I could ask you the same thing! What was that wisecrack about first impressions?"

"I'm sorry. I'm afraid that didn't come out like I'd planned."

She caught the word *planned* and something ugly started to take shape in her mind.

"What I meant to say was your business would get off the ground faster if you could make a better first impression."

She glared at him.

"That is, it would be nice if your work materials were more organized."

More glaring.

"Help me out here, Jessica. You know what I'm trying to say."

She closed her eyes and turned away to calm herself. She was afraid she did know what he was trying to say. And it was becoming obvious the guy had set her up so he could say it.

She turned to face him. "The message is loud and clear. You think I can't impress clients unless I have a building full of inventoried supplies. You don't believe people will give me a chance because I have stains on my clothes and dirt under my fingernails. Well, I happen to think that I clean up pretty nicely. And my work speaks for itself. You may have this big warehouse, but I have the gardens at Sacred Arms. My work was done without the help of a business partner and simultaneously with a demanding dance career. My reputation will win clients no matter what you think.''

Drew reached out and laid a hand on Jessica's arm. She dropped her eyes to the place he touched, but she didn't pull away.

''I'm sorry. Please, can we just back up a few minutes and start over?''

She stood still, head down.

He continued. ''I know you're determined to do everything on your own. And I also know how challenging it can be to recover from an injury. I understand that sometimes it's hard to manage it all.'' He paused. She could tell he was searching for the right words.

''But the mess in the parking lot, the trail of stuff between your car and your front door, and the carts and wheelbarrows all around the compound really bother me. So I was trying, in my bumbling way, to show you how to improve things. I thought maybe if you saw what we've done with a greasy old garage you'd be inspired to find some commercial property. An acre or two with a small building is all you need.''

While he spoke, she stood quietly listening.

"Make a leap of faith, invest in yourself and trust that God is in control."

When she raised her head, she felt tears prick at her eyes.

"If God is in control, He has certainly made a mess of my life. I'm not going to trust my future to anybody but myself, and I *will* have a place of my own someday. The fact is my savings are about to run out and I can't afford anything like that until I generate some new income."

What a fool she'd been to polish her toenails and put on mascara, believing that a man was truly interested in her again. Well, she'd never let him know that.

Kiss or no kiss.

"And that'll happen soon," she insisted. "I just have to get the word out that I'm in business and then it's only a matter of time and effort and a good growing season."

He nodded agreement.

She turned her back to him. She swiped a quick hand through her hair and after a deep breath, faced him with a smile. It was the practiced expression she'd used during performances when her feet were killing her. Most people never knew the difference.

"Would you mind if we cut our tour short? I really have a lot to do this afternoon," she lied. Her heavy plans included walking Frasier down to Grant Park and reading the latest issue of *Georgia Living*.

"Well, there you two kids are." A cheerful Hank

Delgado walked toward them. "The guys told me you had a pretty customer interested in the red '68." He held out his right hand. "Welcome, Jessica."

"Hi, Hank." She shook his hand briefly, glad for the interruption. "Sorry to disappoint you, but I'm just looking around. This is quite a place you have here."

"Thanks. Giving her the nickel tour, huh?" Hank asked Drew.

Jessica thought she caught a conspiratorial look passing between them, but she ignored it, not wanting to overreact in light of what had just happened.

"When's your visitor coming?" Hank said, changing the subject.

"Not for another week yet."

"Well, get out of here and enjoy this beautiful day before I put you to work."

"Do you need me? I feel guilty taking a day off. I can come back a little later."

"No way. You deserve the time to get settled. Go sort some socks or bleach something."

Jessica was drawn back over to the red convertible, and Hank followed. She stroked the canvas top, careful not to touch the shiny trunk.

"It really is a beautiful car," she said to herself.

"It could only be more so with you behind the wheel."

She grinned at Hank's sales pitch.

Drew stepped closer.

"I'm afraid I'm not in a position to even consider

a car like this right now. Maybe I can have one like it in a few years, when I'm established in my second career.''

''Second career?''

''You remember, Jessica does all the landscaping at Sacred Arms. She's hoping to get some additional clients soon.''

''I've applied for a business license under the name Living Colors.'' She shifted her gaze from Hank and looked pointedly at Drew. ''With the gardens at Sacred Arms on my résumé, I don't think I'll have any trouble getting started.''

''I bet you're right. I took a good look around when I was helping Drew move, and you've done some nice work on that old piece of land. I remember all the local fuss when that rich developer Daniel Ellis bought the property and announced he was gonna remodel everything and sell it like town houses.

''People got all bent out of shape over it. But the only reason the school was built on that property in the first place was because it was cheap. It failed because it was in the middle of nowhere, and it sat empty for all those years. Now everything's been restored all around it and Ellis is a rich hero. But you're the real hero, Jessica, for turning those worn-out grounds into pricey real estate.''

She was touched and surprised by his speech. It was nice to know there were strangers who knew the history of Sacred Arms and valued what she'd accomplished.

"Thank you, Hank. I can't tell you how much I appreciate hearing that."

"How'd you get involved with that place anyway?" Hank crossed his arms over his chest and rested faded jeans against a nearby support beam.

"I was one of the first homeowners there. That was almost four years ago and I really couldn't afford the asking price. Valentine had taken me under her wing and wanted me to have the property so much she got the developer to give me a nice discount in return for my horticultural services. I don't actually work for the complex, but I oversee the grounds maintenance and do the new planting myself. It's only been a full-time effort since my professional dance career ended about six months ago." She inclined her head toward her cane.

Hank burst into hilarious laughter. He paused for a breath, smiling broadly at her.

"I love a woman with a sense of humor. There are too many in this world who can't poke a little fun at themselves like that. You, dancing." He rolled his eyes at the image. "That's a good one, Jessica."

"It's no joke, Hank." Drew stood behind her, placing a hand on her shoulder. "Before her accident she was with the Atlanta Dance Theater."

Hank sobered and jerked upright on both feet. "Well, now, I feel like a horse's behind. I thought you were pulling my leg." Discomfort was etched on his face.

"It's okay." She took pity on the man. "I know it

seems unlikely, seeing me today. I have changed a lot, but fortunately this is still the same.'' She held up her grass-stained thumb with pride.

Drew lightly squeezed her shoulder. She knew from their expressions that both men were silently thankful for the graceful way she had handled the gaffe.

With one last glance around, she leaned tiredly on her cane and moved toward the door.

''Good to see you again, Hank.'' She stepped outside into the sunshine.

''Hey, man, I'm so sorry,'' Hank offered as soon as the door closed after her.

''You just took up where I left off,'' Drew said, exhaling his exasperation. He couldn't feel worse. ''I'll fill you in later.'' Drew stepped away and the door closed behind him, too.

They were both buckled in. Before he started the engine he turned to Jessica, hoping to smooth over a rough morning.

''Let's head over to that landscape supply I was telling you about. I thought we'd have some lunch after that.''

''Could I get a rain check on both? I really do have a full afternoon,'' she said, too cheerfully.

''Are you sure that's what you want?''

''I'm positive.''

He'd been wrong. He could feel worse.

Chapter Six

Each time Jessica went to the parking lot to fill the wheelbarrow, the expensively dressed young woman who'd been standing in Drew's bedroom window for the better part of two days watched every move. Compared to her preppy summer togs, Jessica's functional work clothes felt shabby.

Not that she was paying that much attention, but how could she help but notice someone practically stalking her!

"This is crazy," Jessica muttered.

She hefted shovelfuls of pine bark, glad for the years of weight training that had developed strong arms and shoulders.

"Why should I care one bit who's staying at his house? If he wants to shack up with some woman, that's his business."

Drew hadn't spoken to her since their silent ride back from Jonesboro, but that was mostly by her own design. It had been pretty simple to figure out his schedule. An absurdly regimented guy, he was up at six, gone by seven and home in time for the evening news. And, predictably, he got up and went to church on Sunday morning.

Avoiding him took only a little strategic planning. So far, she'd been able to coax Frasier to do his business at times that didn't conflict with her neighbor's comings and goings.

Becky Jo had spoken with him. Jessica knew because she stood in the darkened laundry room with the blinds open at night and witnessed their occasional exchanges. Becky Jo always relayed his simple inquiries about her roommate with a romantic twist. Jessica should never have told her about the kiss.

That kiss. Like a lovestruck schoolgirl, she'd relived it a hundred times. But it had only been part of a plan to get her to clean up her supplies.

Hadn't it?

She looked around at the latest mess with satisfaction, wondering if he'd noticed. Or if he cared. The answer to that question was staring down on her.

"Two can play at this game," Jessica muttered.

She turned, squinted upward, then smiled and waved broadly toward the windows. The brunette with the fashionably short haircut smiled and waved back, obviously pleased by the overture.

As Jessica watched from below, the woman moved to the corner of the window and began cranking open one section of the louvers. Leaning down, she shouted through the opening.

"Are you Jessica?"

Stunned by the question, Jessica just stood, open-mouthed, staring upward.

"I said, are you Jessica? Andrew told me Jessica lives next door with a dog and carries a stick."

Andrew? Stick? This was getting more puzzling by the moment.

"Yeah, that sounds like me."

"I'm not supposed to talk to anybody, but you're Jessica. I think it's okay to talk to you." Her voice was soft and high, her words childlike.

"Sure it is. What's your name?"

"I'm Faith. I'm visiting Andrew."

Jessica exhaled a silent "Oh," unaware that she'd been holding her breath. Faith was Drew's sister. He'd mentioned she still lived with their father, and now the reason suddenly dawned on Jessica.

There'd been a national outpouring of sympathy for Senator Keegan years ago, after the tragic death of his wife. A drunk-driving accident had ended her life and left the senator's only daughter with permanent head injuries.

Jessica smiled at Faith. "Do you want to come over to see my dog? His name is Frasier and he loves company."

Jessica saw her nod at the invitation, but then look troubled.

"I can't. Andrew told me to stay inside and keep the door locked. He never likes it when I talk to strangers."

Of course the girl had been given safety instructions, but Jessica considered herself to be an exception. After all, he'd told Faith about her. Something inside did a small flip-flop at that realization.

"Oh, sure you can. I'm not a stranger. I'll call the shop and tell him you're with me. Come on down and meet me at the front door."

Jessica left her load of pine bark where it sat and made her way inside the building. She'd knocked only once when the door opened to reveal a woman about her own age, with a trusting, open face and eyes the same chestnut-brown eyes as Drew's.

"You have a dog?"

"I sure do. And it's time for his walk. Would you like to go with us?"

The excitement in her smile twisted Jessica's heart into a knot.

"First let's get you out of those nice things. Do you have any old clothes with you?"

Faith opened the door wide to let her new friend in and Jessica's opinion of the brother, who was so protective of this girl, went up a notch.

The front door was unlocked. Drew jumped to full alert. When Faith didn't answer his call, he raced up the stairs. Adrenaline pumping, he made a quick pass through all the rooms of the house before extending his search to the grounds.

He'd hated leaving her alone all day with crafts and videos for company. She did it all the time back home and he knew how quickly she'd get bored at the shop.

When she wasn't in any of the residents' favorite outdoor spots, he offered up a prayer and made a dash for the Commons, thinking she might have wandered there.

"I was afraid something like this would happen when I let her talk me into coming. She's going to be on the next plane back home when I find her." Even as he muttered the words to himself, he knew he'd never have the heart to call an early end to his baby sister's visit.

As he tried first one room and then another, fear began to surface. As well-adjusted as Faith was, she was not equipped to deal with a crisis. In all his years of dangerous military maneuvers, Drew had never panicked. But the thought of something bad happening to his sister, so dependent upon others, brought panic close now.

Hurrying back down the hallway toward his own door, he suddenly thought to enlist Jessica's help in the search. He pounded loudly and called her name. From inside came the sounds of barking and familiar laughter. Jessica opened the door, and there on the floor, surrounded by photograph albums, sat the obviously happy object of his worry.

"Roselyn Faith Keegan! What are you doing here?" His fear turned to anger. She'd disobeyed orders.

Faith's expression changed in a moment from delight to remorse. Her bottom lip began to quiver as tears gathered and then fell. Drew stooped low to fold his sister in a comforting embrace, his anger forgotten.

"I'm sorry, Andrew. I wanted to see the dog." Faith sniffled.

"You promised you wouldn't open the front door. How could you leave the house like that?" He gentled his words and pulled a fresh bandanna from his hip pocket to wipe her tears.

"It was my idea. Really." Jessica defended Faith. "I saw her in your window. I introduced myself and invited Faith over to visit. I didn't think you'd have such a problem with it."

Drew stood. He stepped over the albums and faced Jessica squarely.

"I'm glad you got to meet Faith. I'm sure you can see she's very special to me and I take her safety seriously when she's in my care. Did it ever enter your mind that I might be alarmed to come home to an empty house? Did you even consider leaving me a note, or is that just one more cleanup detail you couldn't be bothered with right now?"

She stood still for a moment. His words resonated in the vaulted room. Then she turned, picked up the phone, pressed the redial button and handed it to him.

On the second ring a voice answered, "Metro Muscle."

"Uh, Hank? It's Drew." He looked suspiciously at Jessica.

Hands on hips, she waited silently.

"Hey, man. I've got a message for you. Jessica called a couple of hours ago and said to tell you your sister is with her."

"Thanks," he said, feeling like a jerk. "I went to see those donor cars and dropped by the bank. Sorry I didn't check back with you sooner."

"No problem. Enjoy the weekend off. See you Monday."

He laid the phone back in its cradle, aware that both women quietly watched him.

"I'm sorry. I overreacted."

"Father says Andrew's a control freak." Faith spoke very matter-of-factly to Jessica.

"Is that so?" Drew contorted his face playfully at his sister. She stuck out her tongue and crossed her eyes.

In a flash Drew dropped to the floor, grabbed his giggling sister in a headlock and affectionately rubbed her crown with his knuckles. He threatened her through gritted teeth.

"You better watch out, Miss Smarty Mouth, or I'll tell Father about those new words you picked up at camp last summer."

Frasier bounced around the horseplay, yapping over the excitement. Drew released his captive and checked to make sure his hair was neat. When he twisted around to tuck in his shirttail, he noticed the opened photograph albums spread across the floor.

The eyes that stared up at him were familiar, but the person was a stranger. Picture after picture of the same pretty blonde adorned the pages. He was embarrassed to have Jessica watching him when the light of recognition finally dawned. He glanced up into her face, her eyes unreadable.

"These are all great pictures. But you look so…" He paused, searching for the right word.

"Skinny?"

"Unhealthy."

"You really think so?"

The disbelief in her voice surprised him. She leaned over to examine the same pictures.

"It's a tough lifestyle. Some dancers go to extremes to stay thin. I just worked hard and was careful about my meals."

"Well, it looks to me like you were careful about *avoiding* meals." He gazed up at her. "I know it was important to be thin for your dance career, but according to these pictures I'd say you were pushing the extreme limits yourself."

Jessica regarded the pictures again, noting the dark circles beneath her eyes and the sharp angles of her cheeks.

"Now that you mention it, I was on the bony side."

"Which may appeal to some men, but I like curves on a woman. Jessica, you're much more attractive today than you were in these pictures."

There it was again. His heart thumping hard in his chest. It had been happening frequently over the past two weeks. And he'd specifically asked for decaf when he'd stopped for coffee earlier. Maybe he'd switch to herbal tea.

Jessica held his gaze after the unexpected compliment, her expression incredulous. It was becoming clear, even to an oblivious male like him, that she struggled with an image crisis. Long weeks in a body cast had taught Drew much about handling that subject. Not knowing whether his brutalized spine would heal, he'd sweated through many nights of imagining life bound to a wheelchair.

During those times, he'd mentally replayed the relentless weeks of combat training, wondering what it had all been for if he ended up broken, only half a man. The mental stress combined with the excruciating physical therapy had been more than he could handle. Only the act of turning his life over to Christ had made it bearable.

"Jessica's taking me to see the dancers." Faith interrupted his thoughts.

"That's if you will allow me. I'm long overdue for a visit to the company and there's a performance tomorrow night. Would you mind if I took Faith?"

His heart continued to thump oddly. Was it anxiety over allowing his sister to go someplace without him or just jealousy because he wasn't included in the invitation? Maybe it was time to have his blood pressure checked.

"You come, too, Andrew. That would be just the thing." Faith tugged at her brother's shoelace. She flashed the family dimples.

He hesitated, wanting to be part of the fun but reluctant to horn in on his sister's new friendship.

"Sure. You're welcome to join us," Jessica agreed. "It will be a nice introduction to the Atlanta artsy crowd."

"As long as you girls are sure I won't be intruding," he agreed.

He stood and held out a hand to help Faith up off the floor.

"Come on, cutie pie. Let's get you home so you can change for dinner." He pulled his kid sister to her feet and, for the first time, noted she was not the well-groomed person he'd left that morning.

"What have you been doing to get so dirty?" He compared Faith's clay-stained T-shirt to its double, worn by Jessica.

"Never mind. Forget I asked."

Jessica was a nervous wreck. She always hated shopping. The day spent at Phipps Plaza searching for something affordable only put her more on edge.

Becky Jo's taste ran from the absurd to the extremely expensive. Having her friend along had only complicated matters. They finally agreed on a two-piece navy suit that accentuated Jessica's tanned arms and shoulders, while playing down her much fuller hips.

Arriving at the theater with the other patrons was a surreal experience for Jessica. For the first time she'd be watching the performance from the outside of the curtain. With all of Faith's questions and exclamations, there was little time to feel nostalgic or sad.

Drew held Jessica's elbow firmly as they made their way down the sloping aisle to reserved seats. Against the physical therapist's orders, she had abandoned the full-time use of her cane, depending upon it only for climbing or stressful activities. This evening probably qualified, but she was determined her visit to the company would not be marred by its presence.

"Jessica says we can meet the dancers afterward."

Faith had been to the theater many times with their

parents, but this would be her first close exposure to a modern dance troupe. The thought of getting to go backstage had her fidgeting with excitement. To focus her attention, Drew opened the program and showed Faith pictures of the company and the ADT board of directors.

Jessica offered bits of personal information.

"Who's this?" Faith pointed.

Looking into the heavily made-up eyes of an extremely thin woman, Jessica forced a smile. What she really wanted to do was snort in disgust.

"That is Amelia Crockett, somebody else I've known for years and hope to avoid if I'm lucky."

"She's not your friend." Faith made everything sound simple.

"No, she's not. She wouldn't let a little thing like friendship get in the way of her social standing, so we've never been friends."

"She sounds like an evil witch."

"Roselyn Faith!"

Jessica coughed behind her hand in an effort to mask a smile. Drew turned away for the same reason, but Faith made no pretense of hiding her own grin.

"Even though I don't particularly like her, Faith, she really has done a lot of good for the company. She's in the program tonight because of her Platinum Patron status. That means Crockett Textiles, her daddy's business, just pledged a lot of money to the ADT. It also means she's around here somewhere, so keep your eyes peeled."

Drew stood to help Faith remove her light sweater.

Jessica caught him making a casual but sweeping glance of the theater. Not once, but twice.

As expected, the first half of the performance dazzled the audience. The ADT had a reputation for athletic dance and innovative choreography.

Faith sat still, her face alight with pleasure, as she watched, spellbound by the performers. Drew hardly said a word, even between numbers. Maybe she'd been wrong to invite him. He must be bored stiff, she thought.

The lights came up and everyone began to head to the bar for intermission.

"Can I have a soda, please? Something lemony. That would be just the thing." Faith left, taking the lead up the aisle.

"Sure," Drew agreed. "I might get something stronger myself."

So he was bored. Jessica began to feel slightly annoyed. After all, he had expressed an interest in attending, so why act put-upon now? Didn't he realize this was her first time back in these surroundings since the accident? She didn't need to be worrying about his feelings when her own were so raw.

By the time they reached the lobby, she was downright ticked off. A bit too briskly, she pulled her elbow from his supportive grip and excused herself to the ladies' room.

Fifteen minutes later, Drew and Faith stood to one side of the lobby, observing the well-dressed crowd, sipping their drinks. A smattering of applause caught their attention.

He glanced toward the noise, surprised to see Jessica at the center of the excitement. Even from a distance, Drew could hear the inquiries and good wishes. She shook hands, gave an occasional hug and nonchalantly handed out business cards.

"That old lady doesn't like Jessica." Faith raised her hand to point.

Grabbing the offending hand and tucking it into his elbow, Drew was once again reminded that what his sister now lacked in IQ points, she seemed to make up with intuition.

A matronly, pug-faced woman stood behind Jessica, looking her backside up and down smugly. She nudged the jeweled arm to her right and the two socialites shared a look down their noses at the fallen star.

Before he had time to think it through, Drew took his sister by the hand and quickly crossed the room. He reached over the heads of the pretentious female observers and gently touched Jessica's chin, possessively tilting her face.

"There you are, darling. I thought we'd lost you in this crowd. I should have expected we'd have to share you with your admirers tonight."

All eyes turned upward at the sound of his voice. The lobby lights flashed several times, signaling the end of intermission.

"Excuse us, ma'am." He directed his comment to Pug Woman. "I need to assist this gorgeous lady back to our seats."

Before Jessica could add words to her questioning look, he caught her hand, drawing her from the crowd. Taking an elbow firmly in each large palm, Drew steered Jessica and Faith away from the curious stares and wondered what in the world had come over him.

Jessica resisted just a bit, forcing him to slow his pace down the aisle. Now and again she stopped briefly to chat and hand out her card.

When they finally reached their seats, she glanced across his chest at Faith and whispered loudly, "Your father's right. He is a control freak."

Standing near the stage at the front of the crowded theater, Drew held Faith's hand after the performance and waited for the foot traffic to thin.

"Drew Keegan! As I live and struggle for breath, is that really you?"

He didn't need visual confirmation. He'd have known the sultry sound anywhere. It was the voice of the woman who'd made him an offer too good to refuse. Somehow he had imagined he'd be more excited to hear it again.

Jessica's eyes widened in amazement when Amelia Crockett pushed past, stepping into what must have looked like a familiar embrace.

Faced with no alternative, he awkwardly returned the hug, flashing a stern face at his sister. Faith, who always spoke without thinking, didn't utter a peep.

"You know each other?" Jessica's voice was little more than a whisper.

"We go way back." Amelia emphasized her comment by keeping her small body pressed against

Drew's side. Eyes for him only, her arm draped tightly around his waist.

He stood still, a hornet's nest of unfamiliar emotions buzzing madly in his head. This wasn't happening as he'd planned, but it *was* finally happening, and he had to make the best of the situation.

So why would he rather be standing in the open door of a transport aircraft at 40,000 feet, preparing to jump?

"Drew and I had very special feelings for each other. Didn't we, honey?"

A cascade of onyx hair framed the exotic face. She hadn't changed—she was pretty as ever and just as bold. He remembered the teenage girl who'd known what she'd wanted, determined to have it all one day.

At that time, Drew's life was mapped out. Deviations from the plan were not optional. He was a West Point senior and regimental commander, and his future was in the military. Everything else was on hold, indefinitely.

He'd left for officer training school and she'd moved on to Wellesley College. Her offer resonated in his memory.

When you get tired of playing army and want some real excitement, come find me in Atlanta.

"Goodness, how long has it been? Eight, nine years?" Amelia stepped back and held him at arm's length, giving him a better view of herself as she openly admired him from head to toe. "If it's possible, you're even more handsome."

The flattery and attention would normally stroke a man's ego. In front of his sister and Jessica, the compliments made him uncomfortable. He needed to get away from her and sort this all out. He relaxed his hold on her hand. She continued to grip his.

"It's wonderful to see you again, Amelia. I've been meaning to get in touch since I moved to Atlanta."

"You *live* here?" He knew her well enough to catch the shift in her tone. She was strategizing. "That's fantastic news. You must join us for supper tonight so I can introduce you to my friends." Amelia spoke exclusively to Drew.

"Speaking of introductions, this is my sister, Faith. She's visiting me from Virginia for a few days."

Realizing she had a green light once again, Faith spoke up. "Why do you wear so much makeup? Father says it's trashy."

"Well, maybe on some women it is, but that's only because they don't know how to apply it. I'd be glad to give you a lesson while you're here and then you can surprise your daddy when you go home. By the way, when will that be?"

"Faith's going to be with me a few more days. I'll call you and we'll get together."

He felt guilty making plans, realizing Jessica was hearing every word. He turned to her. "Forgive me, Jessica. I believe you and Amelia are acquainted."

For the first time since spotting him, Amelia noticed Jessica.

"You!" Amelia's dark eyes narrowed. She whipped around to face him, ebony hair flying. "What are you doing with her?" she demanded.

Drew would have been the first to admit he had

zero experience dissecting the feminine psyche, but this was a reaction he hadn't expected.

"Andrew Keegan, answer me!" Amelia persisted with a spoiled stamp of her designer shoe.

"Jessica is my neighbor. Faith and I are here tonight as her guests."

"Are you aware you are associating with a *murderer?*" The smoky voice shrilled with accusation.

Jessica stepped closer. "That's a lie, Amelia. Adam's death was ruled an accident, and you know it."

"Oh, sure." Amelia glared up at the blonde, taller by several inches. "Is that what you tell yourself at night so you can sleep?" Appraising her opponent, Amelia let out a whistle of disbelief and smiled with satisfaction. "Well, well, well. I heard you'd packed on the pounds, but I had no idea it was this bad."

Jessica didn't flinch at the verbal blow. Drew winced in sympathy, his insides twisting with the revelation. The accident that had destroyed Jessica's knee was the very one that had killed Amelia's brother, Adam.

"I don't have time for your insults," Jessica replied. "Faith and I have people to visit backstage."

"Maybe you need to make time." Amelia wouldn't let it drop. "I'm only saying what everybody's thinking. How in the world could you let yourself go like this? And so soon?"

Jessica squared her shoulders and took a step closer. Amelia stepped back, reaching for the hand Drew had conveniently put in his pants pocket.

"Yes, I've 'packed on the pounds,' as you so astutely point out. I know you're thrilled to finally have a legitimate reason to wag your tongue about me.'' Jessica self-consciously smoothed her hands down the sides of full hips, her gaze searching his face. ''However, a gentleman recently told me he likes curves on a woman.''

Amelia's mouth popped open with a quick little gasp.

Jessica winked at Faith, who'd witnessed the confrontation through wide, confused eyes.

''And now I'm taking my new friend to meet my old friends. We'll leave the two of you to reminisce.''

Drew watched as the two women navigated against the exiting crowd, hand in hand, carefully mounted the stage steps and disappeared behind the dark curtain. He turned a disappointed look toward Amelia.

''Was that really necessary?''

''You can't be serious,'' she snapped incredulously. ''Do you have polite conversation with the drunk who killed your mother?'' Amelia paused, pretending to consider her own question. ''Oh, wait. That drunk is still locked up in prison, where he belongs. But Jessica Holliday is out socializing tonight.'' She pressed a shaking hand over her heart. ''You can't honestly expect me to treat her kindly.''

He exhaled the breath he was holding, understanding too well the depth of her grief. ''I suppose not, but you could at least show some restraint in front of all these people.''

''I am who I am, Drew. I don't go with the crowd, and I seem to remember that was something you liked about me.'' She leaned suggestively against his chest.

"I remember there were other characteristics you appreciated, too."

He put his hands on her bare shoulders and eased her upright. "That's correct. There were many things I liked about you. Even some I thought I could love. But I've changed a great deal since then, so let's not rush. We have plenty of time to explore our memories. Okay?"

"Okay." Amelia tossed her long black hair over a bony shoulder and adjusted the thin strap of her sequined gown. She reached into her satin bag, located a small card and slipped it into his pocket. "Just don't wait too long. We have a lot of lost time to make up."

With that, she reached up and grasped his lapels, pulling his face down to hers. Then she kissed him roughly, a reminder of the past. She patted his breast pocket and smiled at the always-present lump of wintergreen candy.

"You haven't changed a bit," she purred, and made her way slowly up the aisle.

Enfolded in the curtain, Jessica watched. Flushed and warm from the pounding of her heart, she didn't hear the laughter of the friends who entertained Faith. She only heard Drew tell Amelia Crockett that there were things about her he thought he could love.

Chapter Seven

"What do I care if the guy turned out to be a big meathead after all? He's just a neighbor, for crying out loud."

Shaded by an enormous maple, Jessica stood at her potting bench, a sharp spade in her gloved hand. Between muttered comments, she stabbed into a pungent bag of soil and filled a long row of red clay pots.

"But Amelia Crockett, of all people! If he had to be a fool over anyone, did it have to be her?"

Flipping a six-pack of periwinkles upside down, she squeezed the bottom of one small cup, roughly yanked out the delicate bloom and stuffed it into the waiting pot.

"Those must be hardier than they look."

Jessica's head snapped up at the sound of Drew's voice. How long had he been within earshot?

"Excuse me?"

"Those little blue flowers. They must be able to take a lot of punishment."

She watched his eyes travel from her bare feet up to the wrinkled shorts and the old baseball team T-shirt. The breeze caught runaway strands of her ponytail, whipping them softly across her face. She expected an annoyed reaction to her disheveled appearance, but warm cocoa eyes smiled back at her.

Realizing she was indeed crushing another innocent plant, she relaxed her grip. Using the back of a forearm she brushed hair out of her eyes.

"What are you doing here?" She should feel guilty about sounding rude, but she was justified this morning.

"I wanted to thank you again for last night. Faith had a great time. She's been on the phone with Father twice this morning already. She can't stop talking about it. You've really made this visit memorable for her."

"Faith is adorable. She's got spunk, she's full of life and she's sharper than *some* other people I know." She glared at him over the last few words. "Besides, we have a lot in common. I could spend hours with her and never be bored. She's a beautiful person."

Something in his eyes softened. The quiet scrutiny unnerved her.

"So are you, Jessica."

She stabbed out another well for the next periwinkle and wondered if this guy ever said anything she could trust. "Yeah, I felt real beautiful standing next to your girlfriend last night."

"I'm sorry about that." He picked up a spade and shoveled soil into the waiting pots. "I'd forgotten Amelia was prone to step on people's feelings. I thought maturity would have changed things."

She noticed that he didn't correct the relationship reference.

"Oh, don't apologize. She and I were practiced adversaries long before Adam's death. I can handle it— not that I have any choice." She paused, expelled a deep sigh and then resumed planting. "But you have a choice. Don't let a neighborly friendship between us complicate things between you two lovers."

She relaxed her scowl at the blossoms, slowly scanning upward from his trim waist, neatly pressed cotton shirt, freshly shaved face into dark eyes.

"You do love her, right?"

The question hung between them in the warm air.

"Scratch that," she said apologetically. "It's none of my business."

"No, it's okay. I owe you an explanation." Drew tapped the spade against the bottom of his shoe and returned it to the workbench, positioned exactly as he'd found it.

"Amelia and I met during a spring break in New York City the year I graduated from West Point. She was a freshman at Wellesley. Thank heaven we were both smart enough to know we were too young for anything serious."

"Well, you're not too young anymore."

"No, we're not. And I'll be honest with you, Jessica. Amelia is one of the reasons I moved to Atlanta. We were both brought up around politics and know what it takes to make it as a couple in the public eye. If I can work my way into state office, there's so much good I can do for people like Faith, who have very few advocates."

"Why here in Georgia? Why not in your home state where your family is well-known?"

"Mostly because I don't want to trade on my father's name." Drew leaned down and rubbed away a trace of potting soil from his sneaker. "Back home I'll never completely avoid the sympathy attached to him because of my mother's death, or the notoriety that's followed him everywhere since he led those impeachment hearings."

He straightened and fixed her with a solemn gaze. "Here I can start fresh, earn a reputation on my own merit." His voice softened. "This is God's will for my life. He's brought me here for a purpose, and a trusting soldier never deviates from the plan."

"I respect that, Drew," she said, preparing for the worst. "So Amelia's going to be your...*partner?*" It was difficult to imagine the selfish Crockett Textiles heiress taking anything but top billing in a relationship.

"That depends upon a lot of things. She always said we'd make a good team. It seems we're both still unattached and, if the feelings are truly still there, I'd planned to give us the chance we didn't take back then.''

So there it was. Jessica plunged her spade into the moist soil, her heart plunging along with it.

''Well, she's free and you certainly have the pedigree she's been holding out for. Congratulations on finding each other again. The two of you should be very happy together,'' she snapped.

Drew remained quiet as Jessica went through the motions of clearing space on her workbench. She tossed tools into a bucket and noisily stacked empty containers.

''But I want you to know something,'' she continued. ''In spite of what Amelia claims, I'd had nothing to drink the night of the accident. The Crocketts have always refused to accept the truth about Adam.''

''Which is?'' Drew waited.

''That he had a reputation for demanding favors from women. Adam was drunk and I was fighting him off when I lost control of his car.''

She turned in the direction of her weak leg and reached for another bag at her side on the ground. In a practiced movement she grasped the corners of the sack and relied on strong biceps to hoist it upward. The heavy sack struck her recovering leg. The knee collapsed immediately, sending Jessica and her twenty-pound load crashing to the ground.

''Don't move,'' Drew commanded as he dropped to her side, gently examining her leg, checking for signs of new injury.

His warm touch pushed her emotions close to the edge. She swiped his hand away, silently cursing the tears of pain she couldn't hold back.

"I'm fine," she muttered through gritted teeth.

"If you're fine, why are you crying?"

"Because the titanium in my knee feels more like barbed wire right now." She massaged the aching knee and shrugged a shoulder against her cheek to brush away tears. "I probably didn't tear anything loose, but I just added the full-time use of that horrible cane back into my life. What a stupid thing to do."

"Can you stand?" He reached to take both her hands but stopped short of touching, a request for permission in his eyes.

Just like the first time they'd met, she had little choice but to rely upon his support. He pulled her to her feet and presented the cane, which she grudgingly accepted. Then he offered her the ever-present bandanna from his hip pocket.

"What's that for?" She sniffed, needing to blow her nose but not wanting to humiliate herself further.

He gestured beneath his own eyes. "Mascara?"

"Oh, great. How is it that you always see me looking like a frump?" She swiped at last night's eye makeup and then gave a noisy blow into the handkerchief. When she looked up again, he was grinning at her. Not just a sympathetic grin, either. A real one, complete with dimples.

"What's so funny?"

"You're funny. You call yourself a frump when the truth is you're gorgeous." He stated it like a fact. "Jessica, don't you know that?"

She sniffed and rubbed at her nose a final time. "Yeah, well, your life's just chock-full of beauties these days, isn't it?"

His eyes narrowed as he absorbed the comment. He tilted his head to one side, studying her face. Somewhere in that head of his the wheels were grinding.

The dimples relaxed. He seemed determined to press his point. "Forgive me for being so blunt, but underneath the fertilizer you're one of the most appealing women I've ever known."

Drew took the bandanna from her hand and dabbed at her smudged face.

"I couldn't resist kissing you that day," he confessed, "and against conventional wisdom I'm about to give in again."

He leaned down and softly met her lips with his own.

As she closed her eyes and inhaled Drew's fresh scent, she told herself she'd allow this second kiss. But no more. By his own admission, he was not free. The devil take this man for being so straightforward.

It only made him more desirable.

The door slammed and Becky Jo bounded up the stairs, with Frasier yapping at her heels. Jessica quickly swiped away the last tear that dribbled the length of her jaw.

"Valentine heard you were kissing Rambo in full view of everybody this morning! What's up with you two? I thought you said he had a thing with that Crockett chick."

"He does, and if she has any say, they're as good as engaged. It was just a pity kiss after I fell on my backside in front of him."

"No way!" Becky Jo melted onto the chaise lounge opposite the bed where Jessica balanced *The Encyclopedia of Perennials* on her chest. Her knee was iced and resting on a stack of pillows.

"Yes, way. He told me himself. He moved here so they could rekindle their college romance."

"Sorry, Jess. I really thought he was interested in you."

"I thought he might be, too." She sniffed, remembering the tender kiss. "Well—" she became matter-of-fact "—we can safely lay that theory to rest. He's on a mission from God and somehow it's all tied to Amelia."

"How can you say that when you were lip locked with him less than six hours ago?"

"It was only a good-luck kiss."

"Good luck?"

"Yeah, I may need it for my appointment at the *Atlanta Chronicle* with Madeline Shure tomorrow, and Drew will definitely need luck on his side if he plans to get involved with Amelia."

"Do you think he knows that yet?"

"No, but he's a smart guy, so it won't take him long to figure it out."

Becky Jo rolled off the chaise, retrieved her turquoise brocade flats and headed for the door. She turned suddenly and her eyebrows shot up.

"You have an appointment with Madeline Shure? The 'Mouth of the South'?"

Jessica beamed. "Yep. Can you believe it? There was a message from her on the machine when I came back in for lunch. I figured she wanted to print something nasty about me in her Sunday column and she was just calling to get her facts straight. It turns out she heard about Living Colors and wants me to help with her daughter's garden wedding reception."

Becky Jo launched herself across the bed, tossed the gardening volume to the floor and hugged her friend fiercely.

"Wow, Jess, that is fantastic news!"

Badly in need of a hug, Jessica returned the sisterly embrace. It felt good to share her excitement.

"I'd hoped for a nibble from last night's contacts, but this is like grabbing the brass ring! If Madeline Shure is happy with my work, everybody in Georgia will hear about it."

"And if she's not?" Becky Jo frowned.

"I'll have to move to Wyoming. She's syndicated across the southeast and I wouldn't be able to get work this side of the Rockies."

"Well, all she has to do is take a look around Sacred Arms and she'll be sold."

Jessica chewed her bottom lip and played with a strand of the ponytail falling from its rubber band. "I don't think it's going to be that easy. She told me some basic things about the reception plans, and I'll only get one chance to pitch my ideas."

"What does she want?" Becky Jo asked.

"Everything from begonias to butterflies."

"Butterflies? Literally?"

"Literally." Jessica had no idea how she was supposed to pull that off. "If I get the job, I'll be up to my ears in bat guano by this time next week. If I remember correctly, she's all shrub and no flowers, so it's going to be a chore getting that place in bloom. I already have a great source for some incredible pots, if I can afford them."

Becky Jo stood, brushing down the front of her paisley folds. "Well, if anybody can convince blooms and butterflies to appear on cue, my money's on you, girl."

Grateful for the support but not too sure she deserved the vote of confidence, Jessica resolved to make a quick run to Callaway Gardens early the next morning, with a stop at a very special pottery studio on the way home.

Thinking Faith would enjoy the butterfly habitat and the company of the artists, Jessica reached for the phone. Faith answered on the first ring.

"Hi, there. It's Jessica. How'd you like to go with

me in the morning to see a glass house full of butterflies?"

"That would be just the thing. I'll tell Andrew."

Faith neglected to cover the receiver and Jessica overheard the brief exchange. Drew sounded hurt his sister didn't want to spend her last morning with him. Faith suggested he'd be free to make plans with his trashy girlfriend.

Drew countered with the threat, "Well, she may end up as your sister-in-law someday, so you'd better watch what you say about her, especially when you get back home."

A moment of silence followed and then Drew added, "You can go with Jessica, if it's really what you want."

"He says I can go," Faith answered excitedly.

Jessica smiled at the girl's ability to twist her big brother around her little finger. Faith proved there was a difference between sheltered and helpless.

"Great. If you'll wear grubby clothes, you'll get an extra-special treat tomorrow. I'll meet you at your front door at seven o'clock and we'll stop to get doughnuts on the way."

She could hear the big smile on Faith's face as she thanked Jessica for the invitation. She could also imagine the Rhett Butler mustache turned down in a scowl over the same offer.

"Could I speak with your brother, please?"

There was a brief pause before the gruff "Hello."

"Is it really okay with you if Faith goes with me

tomorrow? I didn't mean to intrude on the last day of her visit.''

''No, it's all right.'' He paused, and she heard a big sigh. ''There are some other things I can get done in the morning instead. But she has a five-fifteen flight, so you have to have her home by two.''

''Would you like to come along?'' Now, why in the world had she said that? She needed to focus on her immediate plans, and he was too much of a distraction. ''We're going to stop by a local pottery studio where Faith can participate.''

She held her breath for his answer.

''No, thanks,'' he replied, after a long pause. ''I know how much Faith will enjoy a day out on her own. You two go ahead. I have plenty of other things to occupy my time.''

''Yes, I'll just bet you do,'' Jessica muttered to herself as she turned off the portable phone and resumed her research.

True to her word, Jessica and Frasier were at his door at 0700. The woman waiting at his doorstep was scrubbed as clean as a new penny. Cheap sunglasses held her damp bangs back. A green scrunchy thing bound up her golden ponytail. He knew it was only a matter of time before little baby hairs crept loose from the bunch and danced enticingly around her face and neck.

The ancient red wagon pulled away and only the dog gave Drew a backward glance.

With his morning free, he could either put in a few hours at the shop or ask Amelia to meet him for a late breakfast. Somehow the recycled grease drums in the warehouse were more appealing at the moment.

Thinking he could extricate himself from brunch more easily than he could dinner, he dialed the number on the card still in his suit pocket.

The phone-call mission was accomplished as planned. He hand washed his car before driving the short distance to Amelia's high-rise.

Before Drew's knuckles made contact with the door, it was whisked wide open.

"I thought you'd never get here," Amelia said in a breathy voice. "I've been desperate to have you all to myself." She slithered against him and began to entwine her rail-thin arms around his waist.

He deflected her determined embrace and set her an arm's length away as his eyebrows rose at her bare-midriff attire and seductive greeting. "What's the rush, Amelia?"

"Isn't this what you want?" She pouted.

"What I want is to go to one of those waffle places and order some scattered, smothered, covered and chunked hash browns."

"Not in this life. But we can walk to a little restaurant down the street, sit in the shade under a big umbrella and order omelettes."

Over the meal, Amelia talked nonstop about the many social successes that had followed her college days. Her interest in his military career and the ac-

cident that had resulted in his discharge was only cur-
sory. At least it spared him from sharing the details
he'd just as soon not recall anyway.

"How is it you've remained single all this time?"

She popped an orange section into her mouth suggestively. "I was waiting for you."

Drew chuckled at the obvious lie. "Come on. The
truth."

"Well, it kind of *is* the truth. You know I'm a
straight shooter with very high expectations. I've au-
ditioned a lot of men for the part, but none of them
ever met all the qualifications. If they have the
money, then they don't have the family name. If they
have both, then they're ugly as homemade mud."

He was struck, yet again, by her lack of tact. "I'm
afraid that clearly leaves me out of the running."

"On the contrary." She reached under the table
and lightly scraped her sculptured nails across his
knee. "You can't do better than the Virginia Kee-
gans."

"Let's not forget your number one qualifier. I'm
something of a glorified grease monkey these days,
which doesn't exactly fit into your grand scheme for
us to become a great political force."

"Mark my words, Drew Keegan. Together we *are*
going to be a force to reckon with. My daddy's going
to be so proud," she said wistfully, almost to herself.

In a practiced gesture, Amelia lifted her jet-black
hair away from a slender neck and shook her head

slightly, as if to dismiss any objections to her statement.

"Besides, I have money. I've always had money, so that's never really been an issue. It would have been nice to find a man with his own, but with you as the prize, I'm not complaining."

Beginning to feel like a first-place trophy, he changed the topic back to Amelia. She was more than happy to return to her favorite subject.

So happy in fact, she refused to let him accomplish a gracious getaway. She insisted there was plenty of time and, for a change, showed interest in someone other than herself.

"So—" she drew out the word "—you *are* here to take me up on that offer, aren't you?" Dark eyes gleaming, she hurried on without waiting for his response. "As soon as Father hears this, I'm sure he'll want to properly introduce you to his friends. I'll put together something soon so we can appear as a couple. We can't afford to waste time."

Time! His head snapped down to catch a look at his watch and he jumped to attention. It was past three. Faith would be worried sick.

He tucked several bills under the edge of his plate, grabbed Amelia's hand and hauled her to her feet. "I'm sorry, but I don't have ten minutes to walk you back to your place. If my sister misses her flight, Father will never let me hear the end of it."

"I'll go with you."

It was a statement, not a suggestion. He had a gut feeling it wasn't a good idea, but there was no time to argue.

Still holding hands, the striking couple left the sidewalk café, hurrying down Peachtree Street to the parking garage. Neither one spotted the well-known cap of short-cropped gray hair beneath her signature hat.

Madeline Shure pulled the ever-present notebook from her expensive designer bag and began to jot down observations.

At the insistent knock, Jessica jerked her front door open with enough force to stir the morning's newspaper from its customary spot on the floor. "Where have you been?" she demanded.

"That's not really any of your business, is it?" The voice was annoyingly familiar.

Drew stepped aside to reveal the source of the response. Amelia Crockett.

Jessica couldn't believe her misfortune. After the romp through Callaway Gardens and the messy pottery class, she was a complete wreck and in need of a shower. She mentally groaned, knowing her house was a mess, as usual. The last thing she needed was this unwelcome visitor.

She should be organizing her thoughts for the most important appointment of her life, and instead she was keeping Faith distracted so she wouldn't panic over her brother's whereabouts.

"Actually, I think it is Jessica's business." Drew corrected Amelia and turned to Jessica. "Please forgive me for being so late. I completely lost track of the hour."

"That's my fault." Amelia rested her hand on his arm possessively. "Sorry, babe."

"Look what I made, Andrew!" Faith hurried down the stairs toward her brother. She withdrew a small flowerpot from a paper sack, its exterior a colorful mosaic of broken bits of china. "Jessica took me to the barn full of trees, and she helped me. Isn't it pretty?" Faith held the pot out proudly for her brother's inspection.

Drew briefly admired the offering before stuffing it back in the sack and steering a messy Faith into the hallway. With no time for his kid sister to shower, Jessica knew he'd be sending Faith home to their father grubby but happy.

Tilting toward the living room, Amelia shook her head in disgust. "I see you're a pig in every sense of the word."

Drew's head turned at the insult in time to see Jessica's front door slam, less than a quarter of an inch from Amelia's perfectly chiseled nose.

The next two hours were as emotionally brutal as anything he could remember from Ranger training. Faith's mental maturity was evident in her childlike trustfulness and cheerful manner, but she was surprisingly independent in a competitive situation. From the battle for the car's front seat to the skirmish over who'd stand next to Drew on the escalator, Faith gave as good as she got.

Drew was equally amazed at Amelia's determination to have her own way, refusing to give an inch where most people graciously accommodated his baby sister. His head throbbed like a seventies disco from their loud argument over the radio station, made even louder by the powerful engine and the wind whipping through the open windows.

Faith's brief "I don't like her!" was whispered a little too loudly in his ear as she hugged him fiercely at the gate. From the end of the boarding ramp she shouted "Dad will think Jessica's stick is just the thing," then disappeared into the 727.

"I know she's your sister and she's—" Amelia actually seemed to search for a politically correct word "—limited, but she shouldn't be allowed to talk to people however she pleases."

The old saying "the pot calling the kettle black" came to Drew's mind. Unwilling to point out the obvious and stir up further arguments, he continued his beeline for the parking garage.

In less than forty-five minutes he was free of the still-complaining Amelia, but not before she'd extracted a dinner invitation for later in the week. He was all too aware his pulse was unaffected by the prospect of a date with Amelia, though it raced whenever he spotted Jessica up to her elbows in dirt.

"Lord," he prayed aloud, "I am so confused.

Amelia seems completely wrong for me no matter how much good we could accomplish together. That can't be what You have planned, especially when You've put such a beautiful distraction in my path.''

He drove home feeling as disoriented as the family cat the day it took a few tumbles in the clothes dryer.

Chapter Eight

The welcoming peace of Sacred Arms washed over Drew as he passed beneath the wrought-iron archway. He opened the car door but remained seated, appreciating the sight of the flowering plants all around him and the smell of freshly mown grass. He was hardly aware of the season's supply of pine straw stacked like bales of hay at the edge of the pavement.

The faded red station wagon pulled crookedly alongside his carefully parked pride and joy.

"How about being the first to congratulate me?" Jessica glowed with excitement.

"Shouldn't I be apologizing instead?" He hurried around to open her door.

She took his hand as she stood, shrugging off his offer of an apology. "Oh, don't worry about that. We had a great morning. I was just concerned about Faith missing her flight."

"Well, I feel like I should make some sort of excuse."

"There is no excuse for Amelia Crockett."

Resisting the urge to agree, Drew scrunched his forehead and ran his free hand through short-cropped hair.

"I'm sorry, that was unnecessary," she added.

"You're the one woman who has good reason to be angry with me and you're apologizing. This is too much."

She squeezed the hand that was still holding hers.

"Then let me make it very simple. I just landed my first big job and I couldn't be angry right now if my life depended upon it."

"That's wonderful news!"

He'd come to realize how much this talented woman needed something special to happen in her life. Fighting the urge to wrap her in a bear hug, he made a more respectful overture.

"Will you let me buy you dinner to celebrate?"

Jessica hesitated. "I'd like to accept, but I have so much planning to do."

"Come on. Let tonight be your one indulgence. Besides, I owe you one for taking such good care of Faith," he coaxed.

"Okay," she agreed. "But tomorrow I am officially under deadline to produce spectacular results. I can't afford to disappoint the Mouth of the South."

"Who?"

"I'll explain later." Jessica glanced down at her

shorts, grungy from the morning's excursion. "I didn't have time to get cleaned up before I went to meet with the client, as you know." She gave him a pointed look. "So give me an hour."

"Take more if you need it," he teased.

Jessica smiled and reached inside the car for her cane. "What did you have in mind?" she asked.

"Do you like Mexican food?"

"Are you kidding? I'm a Texan."

"Perfect," he said, meaning it in more ways than one.

Drew and Jessica sat on the patio of the small Mexican restaurant, oblivious to the lively mariachi music. The basket of salted chips went untouched as she told him about her plans for the Shure wedding. He was amazed by the assortment of flowering plants she'd committed to producing.

"How long do you have to get this together?" He wondered if she honestly had any idea how she was going to pull off this extravaganza.

"It's two weeks from tonight. If I work day and night, and subcontract the heavier stuff to the lawn service, I should be able to manage."

"Where will you do all the work?" He envisioned her standing in a greenhouse among all the materials she'd need for such a large undertaking.

"The only place I have. Sacred Arms." Jessica placed a hand on his forearm as he groaned inwardly.

"Now, don't look like that," she cajoled. "I promise it won't be as bad as it sounds."

But she'd already mentioned dozens of containerized gardens, hundreds of plants, a truckload of potting soil. He conjured up a small army of delivery trucks coming and going through the security gate. The thought of all the clutter closed in on him, claustrophobia even in this open place.

Then his practical side took control, making things even worse. He saw the investment in his new home deteriorating like wilted spinach on Jessica's compost pile.

"Can't you rent some temporary space for all that stuff? A warehouse somewhere on the side of town near your client?" He hated the nervous sound of his own voice.

"No, I've already told you, I can't afford it. And even if I could, I wouldn't. I need to have everything close to me so I can work literally around the clock putting these gardens together. I'm going to be searching for materials during the day and then doing the physical work of planting in the evenings. It wouldn't be practical to do it anywhere else."

That only exacerbated the situation. Now he had images of floodlights throwing the moonlit parking lot into a bright state of chaos by night.

Jessica must have thought he wasn't listening to her. She pulled the hair on his arm to get his attention.

"Ouch!" He jerked away and rubbed the sore spot. "Why'd you do that?"

"Because you looked like you were going into a trance. Please stop imagining the worst and give me some credit for being able to run an organized workplace."

Drew's eyebrows shot up and he tapped the side of his head with the heel of his hand as if draining water from his ear.

"Excuse me, I thought I heard you say something about being organized."

"I *am* organized!" She pounded the table for emphasis, sending tortilla chips flying. "You don't have to be Martha Stewart to know where everything is," she insisted hotly. Her gaze fell to her lap, where her hands had wrung the life from a paper napkin.

He watched her struggle to regain composure. The blush that infused her cheeks was terribly appealing. He'd love to see her in a full-blown bad mood some day. He witnessed the red stain spreading across the graceful curve of her throat and wondered if the warm skin there was as soft as it appeared.

He shook off the intruding thoughts and considered for the first time that he might be wrong. Something he seemed to be doing frequently. Maybe she deserved the benefit of the doubt—not that there was anything he could do to change her mind at this point anyway.

Jessica stared him straight in the eye. "I'm sorry I lost my temper. But you don't really understand what's at stake. I only know two things—dance and gardening. And every time I look in the mirror I'm reminded all over again that dance is in the past.''

She held out both hands to him, palms upward. ''What I can conceive in my head and create with these two hands is all I have left. If I'm successful on this job the payoff will allow me to lease property for Living Colors. But the real reward is what Madeline Shure can do for my reputation if she likes my work.''

''Madeline Shure? That newspaper columnist? She's your client?'' Even residents new to the region were familiar with the name.

Jessica let out a big breath and put a shaky smile back on her face. ''That's her. Local folks call her the 'Mouth of the South' because she can't keep anything quiet.''

''Do you think she might be interested in buying an old sports car?'' Drew joked as he scooped chips up off the table back into the basket and motioned to the waiter for a fresh supply.

''She might be. Money doesn't stand between her and anything she wants. Nothing does, for that matter, which is why this job is so important to me.''

A wise soldier knows when to retreat. ''Yes, I can see that. I'll tell you what— I promise to keep my worries to myself as long as you promise to control the mess around Sacred Arms for the next two weeks.'' He extended his right hand.

She eyed it suspiciously. ''And you expect me to trust you?''

"I do," he said without hesitation.

"You realize you're not exactly batting a thousand with me."

She *had* caught him in a couple of less than straightforward situations.

"I do," he repeated. "Give me another swing." He continued to offer his hand across the table. "Deal?"

She took it. "Deal."

They sat in the dark parking lot. Drew was reluctant to leave Jessica's company. He felt a compelling attraction as she plotted her determined plans for independence. Recalling the enticing way her cheeks had colored with excitement when she'd described the wedding project, he warmed inside at the sound of her now, still bubbling over with ideas.

"I'm sorry. You must be tired of listening to me run on about this wedding. Besides, it's getting awfully late."

The inside light of the car flickered on as she opened the door. Before she could climb out, Drew caught her attention by tugging playfully at her silky ponytail. Something he'd been dying to do all evening.

"Actually, I'd like to hear more." Protective feelings surged at the uncertainty in the deep green eyes. "Honestly."

"Well, if you're sure." Jessica glanced toward the light burning in her upstairs windows. "Talking with you all evening has gotten my creative juices flowing. But it looks like Becky Jo's still up, and she'll want me to start over from scratch. Besides, I really need to put up my leg and ice my knee."

"Would you mind if we went to my place instead? I'm enjoying this creative-juice thing, and I can offer you some therapy for that knee."

She gave him that look again. He wondered if Jessica would be so unsure of herself if she knew the confusing emotions she stirred in his orderly mind. Amelia's dark eyes glinted briefly through his thoughts—not as appealing as the jade ones he focused on now.

"What do you say?" he coaxed.

"Sure," she agreed with a nervous sigh. "Got any diet cola in that fancy kitchen of yours?"

"Like a good scout, I'm always prepared."

Half an hour later Jessica sat quietly next to Drew on the deep leather sofa. Her feet rested atop the coffee table. An ice pack slowly melted against her knee and all thoughts of wedding receptions were temporarily banished.

She'd been admiring the long legs that stretched out beside her own. Her insides fluttered at the sight of those legs, tightly encased in denim. She closed her eyes against the desire to reach out and lay her palm on the solid thigh.

It felt so good just to lean back against the soft leather. She should be planning, but the pleasant eve-

ning was a welcome change from the worries of recent months. The cushions shifted as Drew left her
side. She glanced up to see him squat beside a CD
tower.

"What have you got in that massive collection?"

"Everything but jazz. I never learned to appreciate
it."

There was silence as he loaded a disc, and then the
sultry voice of a young Latino starlet floated across
the room. Jessica closed her eyes again, enjoying the
sense of total relaxation.

Drew's words were murmured close to her ear.
"I'm going to refill your ice pack."

An agreeable "Mmm" was her only response as
he padded up into the kitchen.

During the segue into the second song, Jessica
heard the heavy weight of male feet descending the
few steps, crossing the oak floor and stopping somewhere in front of her.

"Will you keep your eyes closed? No matter
what?"

She smiled in her self-imposed darkness. "What
are you up to?"

"Nothing your mother wouldn't approve of."

"In that case, you talked me into it."

He deftly stepped one foot across her legs. She
heard him push aside the heavy mahogany keepsake
box and sit down on the sturdy table. Ice rattled inside
the waterproof pack when he tossed it to the floor.
"I'm going to touch your feet now."

She scrunched her toes up and giggled. "My feet are ticklish."

"I'm not going to tickle them. Just touch them. Okay?"

Jessica's leg jerked involuntarily with the first jolt of sensation, but the immediate relief that followed was worth the effort it took to lean back and keep her eyes closed. She felt a warm hand lift her heel and position it securely atop his knee.

With sure motions he smoothed and kneaded the arch, always sore from so many years of abuse. Warm fingers slipped around and between her toes, coaxing the tight knuckles to pop softly. Work-toughened palms stroked in circular motions against the dancer's calluses, pressing lotion into dry skin.

When he moved to the other foot, Jessica groaned her approval. "As Faith says, this is just the thing."

Drew chuckled agreement.

He followed the same course of relaxing massage with her right foot and then began his slow climb toward her damaged knee. With confident motions he ran his thumbs alternately up the length of her strong calf, murmuring his appreciation for her muscle tone.

When his hands reached the surgical site, he hesitated.

"It's ugly, isn't it?"

"Your incision?"

She nodded, her mind's eye seeing his grimace at the angry red scar, surrounded by permanent staple tracks.

"This little thing?" He blew out a puff of air, a sound of disagreement. "I've seen worse, trust me. Give it two years and it won't be much more than a cat scratch."

"You think?" She was hopeful.

"I'm certain of it."

He placed her heel carefully atop the table and repositioned the ice pack.

Jessica felt his weight on the sofa as he sat beside her, his muscular thigh pressing near her own. Gently his hand eased behind her head to reach for her ponytail. Her thumping heart beat out a rhythmic reminder—he's not free, he's not free. But she didn't resist when he lightly caressed the back of her neck and tugged away the cloth binder.

He buried his fingers in the softness and turned her face toward his. Drawn into his arms, she was spellbound by the power of his embrace.

Her heart drummed faster in her chest. *He's not free. He's not free.* The warning pounded in her ears.

She pulled away.

"I'm sorry to break this spell," she said nervously, "but could I have some ice water?"

"You just had a soda."

"Please?"

He pushed to his feet and busied himself in the kitchen.

"May I borrow your rest room?"

"As long as you don't mind taking the stairs. I'm

replacing the fixtures down here.'' He gestured toward the small powder room.

Jessica eased off the sofa and climbed the flight to Drew's master bath. She splashed cool water on her flushed face and ran his brush through her tousled hair. She stared at her wide-eyed reflection in the mirror, a shaking hand pressed against her chest as if that would slow the frantic beating.

The doorbell chimed downstairs.

Voices drifted upward.

''No, it's okay. You wait right there and I'll take you home.'' Drew insisted.

''If I wanted to go home I'd have given the driver my own address. I went to a lot of trouble to get your security code. I want to stay here with you tonight and get reacquainted.''

Jessica recognized the imperious tone.

Amelia!

Chapter Nine

Flipping off the light and closing the door, Jessica groped in the darkness for the closet and quietly eased inside. Shivering nervously, she kept the door open just a crack to listen.

Drew's voice grew louder as he neared the upstairs landing. Then feet drummed on the carpet as he marched Amelia back down the stairs. "Stop that! Sit down and behave. Just give me a minute."

The closet door opened and closed softly. The overhead light blazed to life. Mortified, Jessica hid like a thief behind a long winter coat.

"What are you doing in here?" he whispered.

"What does it look like I'm doing? I'm trying to save us both some embarrassment."

"I'm sorry. I had no idea this would happen."

"That makes two of us." She pulled the coat closer.

"She shouldn't be here."

"She has a right to be here and I don't."

"Yes, you do. I invited you."

"And now the party's over. Get her out of here so I can go home!" she insisted.

"No. Come out of there and let's go downstairs."

"Are you crazy? She hates me and she'll do everything in her power to get even with me if she finds out we've been alone, together, in your home."

"You have a point," he conceded.

Her head bobbed. "A sharp one. And I've had enough excitement for one day. I need to get some sleep so I can get started first thing tomorrow."

"Listen, I'm going to be gone for the next few days," he apologized. "But I'll talk to you as soon as I can."

"Oh, Captain Keeeeegan?" Amelia was pounding on his bathroom door.

He took a hesitant step toward Jessica. She waved him away, pulled the door closed and clicked off the light.

Jessica stood alone in the dark long after their voices had faded. Tears of frustration filled her eyes.

"Lord, whatever I did as a child to provoke You, isn't losing everything I've worked for and gaining all this weight enough payback?" she demanded, her face tilted toward the ceiling. "How about helping me out here? For a change, can't a guy be there for *me?* I really need to know there's one man in this world I can depend on."

She grabbed the hem of a sweater and swiped at her wet cheeks. Pressing it to her face, she caught the distinctly clean scent of Drew. A sigh, desperate with longing, escaped.

Hearing the low rumble of his car, she crept from the closet and down to the shadowy kitchen. She reached to retrieve her shoulder bag where it sat on a bar stool, her cane hooked over the wicker back. She realized that it was right out in the open.

There was no way it could have been overlooked by the unexpected visitor.

''Amelia, I have to be honest with you,'' Drew insisted as they crossed the threshold into her apartment. ''There's no future in this relationship.''

It was as if she hadn't heard a word he'd said on the twenty-minute drive through late-night Atlanta traffic.

''Let me change and then we'll talk. Make yourself at home.'' She tossed the words over a bony shoulder and disappeared down the hall.

That proved to be nearly impossible. The huge apartment lacked practically everything that fell within his ''comforts of home'' category. There was no television or CD collection. Only a very sophisticated cable sound system that seemed to be permanently set on the jazz channel. There were no magazines, no newspapers and no paperbacks lying about, as he'd seen in Jessica's cluttered but cozy nest.

The place reminded him of a builder's model.

There were signs of life but no signs of living. Seeing Amelia's home, the place that should most reflect her inner self, Drew was certain his decision to end the charade was justified. He wasn't entirely sure of the Lord's plan for him, but he knew God was steering him away from this woman.

After thirty minutes of waiting, his patience had reached its limit.

"Amelia?" he called out.

He cautiously made his way down the hallway.

"Amelia, are you okay?"

When there was still no answer, he began to wonder if she'd fallen asleep. Taught by his mother that a woman's private space is sacrosanct, he knocked lightly on the door. It opened with a whoosh. A slender arm shot out, grabbed him by the bicep and urged him into the heavily scented room.

Amelia was draped in a black silk kimono, a deep V at the throat, tightly belted at the waist. She released him, stepped back and twirled seductively for his approval.

As she moved, the outline of her shoulder blades and the sharp points of her collarbone held his attention. The garment was unflattering. Survival instinct told him to keep his opinion to himself.

"Well?" She obviously expected a compliment.

"Well, I see you've changed. Let's go talk in your living room." He backed into the doorway.

"What's your problem?" She slithered against him, sliding her hands over his chest.

Amelia was a beautiful woman and the unchallenged heiress to her father's millions. She had the education and social background that made her an ideal catch. But everything about her repeated efforts to seduce him felt terribly wrong.

The cloying scent of her designer perfume stung his nostrils. He closed his eyes for an instant while his subconscious conjured up the memory of shampoo and potting soil. His heart hammered at the thought. If he had any doubts left, they fled at that moment.

He turned her by the shoulders and steered her down the hall toward the leopard-print sofa. After he gently forced her to sit he reached for a cashmere throw and draped it over her exposed legs. Crossing the room in long strides, he grabbed a dining-room chair, positioned it directly in front of her, sat and leaned forward.

"I need to settle this tonight, Amelia. I've given control over my life to God and I'm certain this is not the kind of relationship He wants for me."

Dark eyes flashing, Amelia sat on the edge of the sofa and tossed the blanket onto the floor.

"Since when do you give up control of anything? If I recall correctly, your whole life has been built around being in control. Busting your tail at West Point and in the army so you could hold rank, all that Ranger and Air Assault training to learn your specialty, all the time you spent building a reputation so you'd be respected as a leader. A man in control. And now you want to give it all away?"

Drew straightened in the chair, surprised she'd paid any attention to his military background.

"Don't you understand the rest of the country will see all that experience and potential, too? Drew, you're a natural for the political arena. With your father's guidance and my father's financial support, there's no chance you can lose."

She reached across the space between them and squeezed his hand. "And with me at your side, we'll be unstoppable."

When he didn't argue, she must have taken that as a positive sign, and she rushed on.

"The timing couldn't be better, Drew. For years Nate Gadston had planned that after retirement he'd mentor my brother. Now the senator's free, but Adam's gone. We can step right into the best political guidance in Georgia. Inside of ten years we'll be ready for a Senate seat. And beyond that, well, that would be up to us."

He stared at Amelia, amazed at the passion in her voice as she put words to her own ambitions. He glanced down to where she still held his hand. There was no warmth in the touch.

"Amelia, Faith is the only reason I'm considering public service. If I can help make the future more secure for my sister and people like her, then it will all be worth it."

"There you go. We already have our platform for our very first campaign." She lifted her shoulders and her eyebrows in an anything-goes manner.

He paused, considering his next statement. "Faith will need a home when our father's gone. Where do you expect her to live?"

"Well, certainly not with us, although a retarded sister would definitely be useful during a campaign."

Drew was up and towering over Amelia so quickly that she leaned back against the sofa cushion to escape his glare.

"My sister's condition is the result of a head injury. She is one of the bravest and most sensitive people I've ever known and I would never put her on display for personal gain." He straightened and took a step back. "I'm sorry, Amelia. It was foolish of me to even consider this seriously."

"You're really going to throw in the towel so quickly?" she asked, eyes wide, clearly stunned by his decision.

"It's more like reading the handwriting on the wall," he replied. "I misjudged this situation completely. I was crazy to even consider that a relationship as important as marriage could be treated like a business arrangement."

"That's where you're wrong, Drew. More marriages would succeed if they were set up like a business deal. Happily ever after is just a fantasy. You have to have a plan, and the one my daddy is putting together for us is a sure bet."

"I'm not a betting man." He released an exasperated sigh. "But I am a tired one, so I'm leaving."

"What time are you picking me up Wednesday night?"

He turned at the front door, wishing his grip on the situation was as tight as his grip on the knob. "Listen to me, Amelia. I'm not going to pick you up on Wednesday or any other day. We're not going to see each other again. It's that simple."

"Oh, no, it's not. What am I supposed to tell Daddy? He's already approached the governor about a power breakfast to introduce you."

"Tell him I'm sorry. For whatever trouble I've caused you, or your family, I apologize. But for me it's not about power."

She crossed her silk-clad arms, tilted her head and smiled. "It's always about power."

Drew rested his elbows on the top of his desk, his hands clasped with fingers laced as he mentally prepared for the conversation to come. After a sleepless night he was even more certain of his decision. He'd prayed his father would see it the same way.

"Marcus Keegan here."

"Father?"

"Andrew!" There was pleasure in the senior statesman's voice. "It's so good to hear from you."

"Thank you, sir. I'm surprised Faith didn't answer."

The older man chuckled. "I am, too. The telephone seems to be her primary interest these days. She insists on answering every call herself and she's become quite good at taking messages for me when I'm out. What's up, son? You're calling rather early this morning.''

Drew checked the time, understanding the statement. Their conversations generally took place in the evening when both men felt the need to talk over the day's accomplishments.

Better than anyone else, Drew knew the extent of his father's grief over the loss of his wife twelve years earlier. While a junior at West Point, Drew had wanted to come home and help with fourteen-year-old Faith's recovery and to complete his studies at a local college. His father wouldn't hear of it. Their longtime housekeeper had become Faith's full-time caregiver. Marcus had managed to complete another full term before retiring, and Drew had stayed at West Point.

Not a day went by that he didn't remember and miss his mother's indomitable spirit.

''I know it's still early. I've been at the shop since daylight and I'm about to get on the road.''

''How's everything going, son?''

''Quite well, actually—just not as we'd expected.''

''You definitely have my attention.''

Drew could envision his father leaning back in his executive desk chair.

''Are you and Amelia ready to make an announcement?''

Here it was, one of the few moments in his life when he just couldn't live up to his father's expectations. Drew thought he might be sick. His chest expanded with a deep breath to steady his voice.

"That's not going to happen, sir."

"So Raymond Crockett wants you young people to hold off awhile? Makes sense not to rush Southern conservatives into accepting a new kid into their club."

"No, sir, that's not what I meant. Amelia and I won't be making an announcement at all. We won't even be seeing each other again." As he spoke, Drew fiddled with a pen between his fingers—anything to occupy his nervous hands.

Marcus's voice moved to the same soft, censuring tone that had effectively unnerved several speakers during the now-infamous impeachment hearings.

"Son, if Amelia's got cold feet, that's no surprise. You've only been in Atlanta a short while. She might need a little more time to get used to this whole arrangement."

"Sir, I'm the one who ended it." Drew waited a moment, knowing the reason was expected to follow immediately. "I'm interested in another woman."

The senator was so quiet that Drew wondered if the connection had been broken.

"Sir, did you hear me?"

"Yes, I believe I did. How did this happen?"

"It was completely unexpected. Jessica's my neighbor."

"Excuse me, is this the woman 'with the stick' that Faith has talked about so much?"

Drew smiled sadly at his sister's description. Remembering the right word to describe an object was one of Faith's ongoing challenges.

"Jessica injured her knee in an accident last winter. She's still using a cane as she recovers."

"How does she figure into our plans, Andrew?"

Our plans.

For the first time in his life, Drew had a plan not developed by committee.

"She's changed everything for me, sir."

"And what happens when you don't stick to a plan, son?"

Drew knew where this was headed. "You stray off target."

"Exactly. Now we need to discuss options to get back on track. Get back with the plan. A lot is riding on your alliance with the Crockett family. How much damage control will we need to do while you put this right with Amelia?"

"Father, there can never be anything between Amelia and me. We're just too different."

"Your mother and I were different, too, but we made things work."

Drew had known this wouldn't be easy.

"You don't realize it, but you insult Mom by comparing your wonderful marriage with the farce of a relationship I'd have with Amelia."

"I guess I'm not completely surprised," Marcus said with a sigh of resignation. "You know, Faith did return from her visit pronouncing Amelia to be rather unpleasant.''

Drew patiently waited through a long pause.

''Tell me about Jessica,'' his father asked. ''Who are her people?''

''Her mother's a seamstress. She lives in east Texas. Jessica's parents are divorced and she lost contact with her father years ago.''

''What's her line of work?''

''Until last December, she was with the Atlanta Dance Theater. That's when she had the accident that left her slightly disabled.''

''And now? She's looking to latch on to some nice, available guy who might support her?''

Drew's patience was being tested.

''Please don't be crude, sir.''

''I'm sorry, Andrew. But this is an unexpected pill you're asking me to swallow. You have the opportunity for entry into state politics through one of the most connected families in the South and you're throwing it away for an out-of-work dancer. That doesn't sound like Captain Andrew Keegan to me.''

Drew wanted to disagree, but he hardly recognized himself these days.

''Jessica is not out of work. She recently started her own landscape design business.''

''Andrew, is there no chance you can reconcile with Amelia?''

''None at all, sir.''

His father's deep sigh punctuated the statement.

Drew knew the next step would be to brainstorm a backup plan.

"What we need, son, is a backup plan. I'll talk to Nate Gadston tomorrow and arrange a meeting for you. As long you're not ending things on a sour note with Miss Crockett, I believe I can still persuade Raymond to throw his support your way."

Drew sank into his office chair and stared at the ceiling tiles as he searched for the words that had to come next.

"Father, Amelia and Jessica are acquainted, and unfortunately there is some very bad blood between them."

"Oh, I can't imagine Raymond Crockett allowing his daughter's petty jealousy to overrule sound political decisions."

Drew swallowed and prepared to twist the knife.

"It's much more complicated than that, sir. You recall that Adam Crockett was killed in an automobile crash last year. Well, Jessica was the woman driving Adam's car the night of the accident."

Drew heard the chair knocked back as Marcus Keegan came to his feet at the news.

"What? You've become involved with the woman who killed Raymond Crockett's son?"

Drew stood as well, gripping the phone with his left hand, making a tight fist with his right.

"Jessica did not *kill* anybody. She took the wheel because the guy was too drunk to drive his own vehicle and she lost control of the car when he jumped her.''

''That's quite a story.''

''It's the truth.''

''The truth can set you free or it can ruin your life. Andrew, I strongly advise you to reconsider this involvement before it's too late.''

''It's already too late, sir.''

''And what's that supposed to mean?''

''I think I'm falling in love with her.''

Weary from a sleepless night and exhausted after a fourteen-hour day, Jessica tossed back the quilt and slid between the cool sheets. The phone jangled on the nightstand. Too tired to answer, she let it ring.

''Are you gonna get that?'' Becky Jo called from the guest room. Jessica glanced at the bedside clock. Ten-fifteen. It could be important.

''Hello?''

''Jessica?''

''Faith?'' Jessica smiled at the familiar voice.

Burrowed beneath the covers in search of his sock monkey, Frasier looked like a lump roaming under patchwork covering.

''Hi! Father said it wasn't too late to call you.''

''Of course not. You can phone me any time. How are you, Faith? Did your dad like the pot you made?'' Jessica recalled Faith's face, scrunched in concentration as she worked.

''Yes, we planted mint in it.''

"That's perfect. You can set your pot in the kitchen window and cook with the mint for months."

"That's what Father said."

Jessica flipped the covers up at the end of the bed and scooted Frasier out with her foot. He dragged his monkey to her side and snuggled down for the night.

"And," Faith continued, "he said he needs to talk to you."

Jessica sat up in the bed, pulling the covers tight over her pajamas. "Now?"

"Yes. Just a minute, I'll get him."

The thought of Marcus Keegan about to pick up on the extension at his home in Virginia sent her pulse racing. Like millions of other Americans, she'd watched the hearings and marveled at the effect his quiet words had had on the president of the United States.

"Miss Holliday?" His voice resonated with authority.

"Yes, sir. Please call me Jessica."

"Thank you for taking our call, Jessica. It's late so I won't keep you long."

"Not at all, Senator. Is there something I can do for you or Faith?

"Since you asked, there is, actually. I'm not a man who minces words, so I'll come right to the point. I'm grateful that you've befriended my daughter. She's a wonderful girl and she can't stop talking about you and your dog."

Jessica relaxed, releasing a pent-up breath and allowing her shoulders to slump.

"The problem is that I understand you're involved with my son."

Once again she sat ramrod straight. "Well, we're neighbors but nothing more than that, sir. Faith may have exaggerated our friendship."

"I must confess, Miss Holliday, I'm glad to hear that. You see, Andrew has some very important goals to accomplish over the coming year. Unwanted distractions could prevent him from staying the course. Do you follow me?"

"I think so, yes." She glanced toward the cheval mirror, squinting at the mess she presented with hair bedraggled and cheeks sunburned from the day's work.

"I would consider it a personal favor if you would bear that in mind."

She rolled her eyes heavenward. *I can't catch a break with You, can I?* She dipped her forehead and massaged the bridge of her nose. "I'm certain I won't have any problem remembering that, sir."

"Very well. I'll tell Faith you said good night. Thank you for your time, Miss Holliday."

"It was my pleasure," she said to the buzzing dial tone.

Chapter Ten

"Jess, wake up! You've gotta see this." Becky Jo's excited voice carried up the stairs.

Jessica rolled slowly off the bed and glanced at the clock. She staggered into the bathroom to brush her teeth and stepped back into the shorts she'd taken off only five hours earlier.

"Jessica!"

"I heard you!" she shouted, taking her time.

Frasier welcomed her with his endearing doggie grin.

"Good morning, buddy. What's new?" She stooped to push the soft white hair out of his eyes.

"I'll show you what's new. Look at this!" Becky Jo shook the newspaper triumphantly in her friend's direction.

Jessica reached past the extended paper into the cabinet for her favorite cobalt-blue mug.

"Read it to me. My eyes refuse to focus at this hour."

Becky Jo made a production out of holding the page at arm's length and cleared her throat as if preparing to present a prestigious award.

"'Luck is changing for the former darling of the Atlanta Dance Theater. Once down, but certainly not out, Jessica Holliday is fighting her way back into the spotlight with her new custom gardening venture, Living Colors. If you see her red wagon racing through Buckhead, kindly get out of her way. There are thirteen days and counting till my daughter's wedding!'"

Coffee sloshed as Jessica set her cup down hard and grabbed the page. With sudden twenty-twenty vision she scanned the article, repeating the words aloud, unable to believe her luck.

"Wow! I could never afford to buy publicity like this! Bless you, Madeline!" She kissed the page and hugged it to her chest. Still smiling broadly, she read the article another time, continuing down the column in case she'd missed some further mention of Living Colors.

Two paragraphs down, another familiar name caught her eye.

"Has the persnickety Amelia Crockett finally found her man? The textile heiress was seen laughing it up and holding hands with a hot-rod-driving hunk this weekend. It's about time she hung up her hoops and left the ball to the younger belles."

The reference to Amelia's propensity for competing with the debutantes would have been hilarious under other circumstances. Jessica found no humor in the social jab, only further confirmation that Drew was a man on a mission to reconnect with his past. Last night had been only a blip on his radar screen.

Pulling the scissors from the utility drawer, she carved out the blurb about Living Colors, which she taped to the refrigerator. Flinging the rest into the recycle box, she headed for the front door.

"Come on, Frasier. I think there's a fancy tire in the parking lot that needs your attention."

"You've got to work with me on this, Sam," Jessica pleaded.

She'd been at the privately owned nursery for hours, gathering the necessary supplies, continually adding to an expensive purchase order. It was a favorite haunt where she could be sure of finding just the right plants for her projects, and Sam Harrelson was always willing to order them for her.

Until today.

"I can't," the owner of the nursery replied helplessly. "You know I'd like to, Miss Holliday, but my supplier makes me pay up front 'cause this is a family business. I have to protect my cash flow."

"Can't you just extend credit to me for a few weeks? I've always paid my bill on time."

Sam scratched his gray head. "Yes, ma'am, I know. But this here's the biggest order you've ever placed. I can't just let you waltz away with thousands of dollars worth of my flowers. What guarantee do I have that you'll be able to pay me in a few weeks?''

As desperate as she was for the supplies, Jessica understood Sam's concern. In his place she'd be asking the same question.

Make a leap of faith. Invest in yourself and trust that God is in control.

Drew's words echoed in her memory. A leap of faith. Invest in yourself. God is in control. Nice platitudes from a guy with no financial worries of his own.

''What does he know about dire straits? He owns a successful business. All I own is my home,'' Jessica muttered under her breath.

''You say something, Miss Holliday?'' The elderly man tapped his hearing aid.

''I said all I own is my home,'' she repeated, a frightening idea starting to take shape.

Her home. Sacred Arms. She shivered in the hot sunshine at the thought of losing her connection to the incredible security of the place, not to mention the extraordinary beauty she'd created. Along with her seedlings, she'd sown a part of herself into the land.

Make a leap of faith. If she didn't make Living Colors work she wouldn't be able to afford the mortgage on her place anyway.

''Hey, Sam, what if I put up something of value as collateral for the supplies?''

He glanced past her toward the gravel parking lot.

"I hope you're not talking about that wagon of yours. I've already got an old pickup for hauling trash and such."

Jessica winced at the insult to her precious Ruby.

"No, I know my car's not worth much." She drew a deep breath and hurried on before she lost her nerve. "But I do have some equity in my home at Sacred Arms. You've made deliveries there for me many times, Sam."

"Oh, yes, ma'am. Beautiful place you've got there."

"Would you be willing to accept my home as collateral?"

Sam spit a dark stream of tobacco juice into a paper cup while he considered the offer. He shook his head. "I don't want to put you out of your place, Miss Holliday. I just want to get paid for my plants."

"You will, Sam. You will. But this way you'll have peace of mind knowing your family business is protected. It's time I took a leap of faith."

Sam squinted hard at his customer, finally extending his weathered right hand.

"You've got yourself a deal, ma'am. Take whatever you want, but don't hurt your knee with any leaping. Not on my property, anyway."

The old barn, cleverly converted to a studio and gallery, sat a few hundred yards off the road, back in the Georgia piney woods. Funded by the owner's profits from her private sales, Helping Hands made free classes possible for physically and mentally challenged adults. Each mosaic pot they created was unique, wrapped in a colorful mixture of broken tiles and bits of china and stoneware.

"These are perfect, Gail. I can't wait to see Madeline Shure's reaction when I show her the samples."

"Jessica, I don't know how to thank you for taking a chance on us." Gail Tinker's eyes glowed from the proposal. "If you can get our pots in front of that crowd, we can find the funding we need to keep the classes going. Otherwise, I have to turn these special people away after this summer. With the downturn in the economy, I can eat or offer classes, but I can't afford to do both."

Jessica watched the concentration on the faces of the artists as they drew patterns on the terra-cotta planters, selected fragments of glass and glued them into place. Faith had loved the process. Gail had helped Faith, calmly coaching her through the work of arranging the jagged bits of color. Planted with a cascade of mint, it would be a jeweled treasure chest of fragrant green sprigs.

Closing her eyes, Jessica envisioned the Shures' monochromatic garden transformed into a rainbow of color. The Helping Hands containers, artfully filled with Sam's flowers and foliage plants and accented with delicate florist's ribbons, would provide the one-of-a-kind backdrop Madeline envisioned for her daughter's reception.

"Are you sure you can provide enough pots? This

is going to be a major undertaking and I have to start right away.''

Gail turned toward her studio and motioned for her guest to follow. Jessica gasped with delight at the contents of the storage room. It was the mother lode. Mosaic containers of every shape and size were stacked high against the walls.

''We've been collecting them for over a year, hoping for the opportunity to have a proper fund-raiser.''

Jessica's heart beat faster at the thought of having so many charming pots, each one an individual masterpiece, lovingly fashioned by caring hands. She impulsively hugged Gail in delight.

''This is going to be a huge success, Jessica. You can take that to the bank.''

''I hope you're right,'' Jessica answered. Her excited heartbeat shifted to a nervous drumming. ''Otherwise there'll be nothing for either of us to take to the bank.''

By noon on Wednesday, Helping Hands had delivered two pallets of carefully chosen pots of various shapes and sizes. In keeping with the wedding's color scheme, Jessica's plan called for sponging on golden highlights and accenting each with matching satin ribbons. Then the pots would be filled to overflowing with all the flowering plants in season.

Adding some expensive silk blooms would take a bite out of the remaining cash, but in her mind's eye she saw the end result and knew it would be just the touch to satisfy the Shures' expensive taste. Selling Madeline on a complete overhaul of her boring box-woods would be the next project, once the wedding job was successfully in the bag.

Jessica estimated a full week of working nights to get the pots accented. For the sake of style and con-sistency she was determined to do them all herself. Bless her heart, Becky Jo had offered to help, but Jessica still had a vivid memory of the shared college apartment they'd painted together during their soph-omore year.

No, Jessica would do this work alone, placing her special signature on each and every container garden.

She was standing in the parking lot at three o'clock, exhausted and hungry, when the gates swept aside for the gleaming white sedan. She huffed a big sigh of frustration, knowing that an impromptu visit from Valentine would require at least an hour of nonexis-tent time. There was no chance for escape. She pulled off the gloves she was using to unload gallon buckets of fragrant lemon-yellow daylilies and perched herself on the edge of her wagon's open trunk.

Valentine approached in her usual crisp linen and fashionable high heels. She looked Jessica up and down, shaking her head in dismay.

''Jessica, dahhhlin', you look a fright.''

Jessica hadn't checked her reflection since Monday and suspected her perfectly coifed friend was accu-rate. She pulled a tattered bandanna from her hip pocket, dabbed at the sweat on sunburned cheeks and then twisted it around her forehead, Willie Nelson style, to hold the damp bangs out of her eyes.

"Pardon me if I'm not dressed to receive visitors." The tone was a little too sharp and the rumble of her stomach a little too loud.

"Oh, honey, I didn't mean to be tacky." Valentine lovingly tucked stray hairs behind Jessica's ears. "You'd be gorgeous in a cottonseed sack. It's just that you're back in the limelight again and you have to dress for the part you want."

"Well, today I'm dressed for the part I have." Jessica smiled tiredly.

Valentine didn't return the smile. "Yes, I suppose you are, and that's the problem."

"What problem?" She rose to her feet, sensing trouble.

Valentine put a gentle hand on Jessica's shoulder.

"Dahhhlin', I didn't say anything about this when you came up with your idea to start Living Colors from your home because I never dreamed there'd be a complaint. But now there has been, and I'm very sorry to have to remind you that Sacred Arms has a strict covenant preventing an owner from operating a business from the premises. You have to move all this stuff immediately and agree to relocate your business within thirty days."

"Or?" Jessica steeled herself for what came next.

"Or risk legal action by the homeowners association against you and Living Colors. But it won't come to that, dahhhlin'. We'll satisfy the complaint and find a place for everything."

A place for everything…and everything in its place.

The message was a jackhammer blow to Jessica's senses.

"You said there's been a complaint? By whom?" She gripped the dirty work gloves as she tried to keep her temper in check.

"Oh, child." Valentine's in-charge demeanor slipped for a moment. "I just knew you'd ask that and I'd rather not say."

Jessica swallowed hard and fought the urge to throw the gloves on the ground and stomp on them.

How dare Drew promise he'd keep his worries to himself, then turn right around and make a complaint to Valentine!

So much for asking God for one man she could trust.

Pushing away the desire for a good old-fashioned tantrum, Jessica took several deep breaths and shook off the burning feeling behind her eyelids. The ache in her gut inched upward into her heart, the pain of being deceived much worse than the hunger for food.

"It's okay, Valentine. I have a pretty good idea for myself, so I won't put you on the spot."

The older woman sighed with relief. "I appreciate it. Now, let's not bother our pretty blond heads with that. Let's figure out how we're going to get you out of this—" she motioned toward the skids of materials that had been delivered in the past few days "—mess. Now, here's what I was thinking."

Valentine continued to talk, but Jessica had tuned her out.

For the first time in recent weeks, she began to feel a creeping sense of panic. Even after the accident she'd possessed the confidence that she'd make it on her own. In the back of her mind she'd always had a plan to get Living Colors off the ground. There just hadn't been money to fund the plan. And there still wasn't.

Once the checks cleared for the paint and floral supplies she'd purchased, there would be next to nothing in her account. Her last disability check would cover the mortgage and utilities. Becky Jo already paid for all their food and she refused to have it any other way. At least Jessica wouldn't starve, although she thought she could probably live for weeks on the fat stored in her thighs.

There was no time to go through the bank for a small business loan. That could take weeks and she had only days.

Valentine was still talking and gesturing toward the Commons. Jessica glanced up at the spectacular stained-glass windows and felt heartbreak for the second time that hour.

"Well, if you've got a better idea say so. But don't just sit there looking like you want to cry, while I work myself into a frenzy out here in this heat!" Valentine stood in a double huff, both hands on her hips.

"What?" Jessica put aside her private worry and focused on the charming pink face. "I'm sorry, Valentine. Let's get inside before you sweat all over that expensive suit."

"Honey, a lady never sweats. She glistens. Anyway, will you take my money or not?"

"Take your money?" Jessica suddenly realized her friend had been offering financial help. "No, of course not." She shook her head emphatically.

"Well, for pity's sake, why not? It's not as if I can't afford it, and I feel partially responsible for allowing you to get into this situation in the first place. And it wouldn't have to be a loan—you could let me be your partner."

Jessica hesitated. The temptation to let Valentine help was appealing. But the idea quickly turned sour at the thought of risking a friend's money, especially one so dear.

She took Valentine's immaculate hands in her dirty ones and gazed with gratitude into the lively gray eyes. "You will never know how much I appreciate your offer. But I'll have to find another way. You believe in me, don't you?"

"What I believe is that, right after me, you are the bravest, most resourceful woman this side of the Mason-Dixon line. And you're stubborn as a male mule, so I won't try to change your mind. Just know you only have to say the word and the money is yours."

Jessica's eyes clouded with unshed tears in response to the older woman's kind words and generous offer. She pulled the sweaty bandanna off her head and made an excuse to swipe at her nose. "I guess the pollen this year is finally getting to me."

"Which is exactly why plan B will be a double blessing." Valentine beamed.

Jessica stuffed the soggy rag back into her hip pocket. "Plan B?"

"Dahhhlin', didn't you hear a thing I said earlier?"

Jessica's head was beginning to pound from the confusion.

Valentine went on. "I guess not. Well, let's go, then." She motioned for Jessica to follow. "I'll show you what I had in mind and this time I won't take no for an answer."

Valentine turned and headed across the parking lot, leaving Jessica no choice but to grab her cane and fall in behind the determined steps.

Well after dark the thunder of the vintage hot rod filled the parking lot. As was his new custom, Frasier barked at the sound and pleaded for a walk. Tonight Jessica obliged him, glad to get the confrontation over and done. The emotion and activity of the afternoon had physically drained her, but she needed this closure before she could rest.

Drew was a neighbor. Nothing more. He *and* his father had seen to that. They'd both made it clear that Drew's interests and loyalties lay elsewhere. She felt foolish, misreading his signals, making too much of the intimacies that were certainly nothing to him.

She'd rehearsed clever insults that would make him believe she felt the same. She'd even tried a few times to convince herself it was true. But remembering his tender kisses only served to make the memories that much sweeter, and that much sadder because they were special only to her.

Wondering what had changed since he'd left, Drew stopped halfway between the garage and the building. Sensing something was out of place, he stood still and gave his home a sweeping reconnaissance. The halogen lights were shining overhead. The wrought-iron gate was firmly closed. A light breeze stirred the crape myrtle.

Jessica's car was neatly parked, the area around it tidy, the recent effort of a leaf blower.

Neat? Tidy? Words he'd never associated with Jessica before suddenly made his heart race. Something was terribly wrong.

The heavy security door fell shut behind the small dog, struggling to drag his resistant owner to the parking lot. Throat thick with emotion, Jessica abandoned her plan to confront Drew. She yanked on the leash and turned away, forcing Frasier in the direction of the lawn.

"Jessica? Wait," Drew called out.

Without a backward glance, she continued on the path that led beyond the pond to the vegetable garden.

"Jessica? I haven't seen you in days, and we have something important to discuss."

The shih tzu refused to cooperate any longer. He strained hard against the leash. The delay gave Drew the few seconds he needed to catch up.

Confronted by the source of her pain, Jessica's well-rehearsed, snappy one-liners fled. She spoke over her shoulder, refusing to face him. "I can't think of anything we could possibly have to say to one another."

"For starters you could tell me what happened to all the stuff in the parking lot."

She turned to him, fighting mad. "It's gone. It's all been moved. You won't ever be bothered by it again. And if your plan works, the same thing will apply to me."

He stood tall, fisted hands on hips, disbelief on his face.

"Would you please explain what you mean by that?"

"I found out you complained, even after you promised you'd give me time to get through this job."

"What?" Drew's head popped back, as if he'd been struck on the chin. "What are you talking about? And how did you come by this information?"

"Valentine told me there was a complaint. Nobody else has ever had a problem with my activities before you came along, so it was pretty easy to figure out. You gave your word. You even shook on it. So much for the integrity of you ex-military guys."

"Now, wait a minute—" Drew stepped forward.

"No, you wait a minute." Jessica stepped up as well, punctuating every third word with a blunt index finger to his chest. "I trusted you to give me a chance to get my life back on track. And now I have to choose between my home and the only way I know to make a living. But I've done the best I can to put your worries to rest, Captain Keeeegan," she mocked. "You can sleep well knowing your investment is safe."

Breathing deeply and struggling for control, she turned and resumed her determined march with Frasier, for once in quiet cooperation.

Chapter Eleven

Drew froze, watching her proud back as she turned the corner and disappeared behind the stone wall. He stood alone in the quiet darkness, trying to make sense of what had just happened.

Lord. He looked upward. *Why did you make women so hard to figure out?*

He knew leaving town had been bad timing after the fiasco at his house, but he fully meant to explain everything and make it up to Jessica, if only she'd give him the chance.

This was out of control. It was a sickening sensation he'd known very few times in a life of being in command. Giving God dominion over his life was the hardest thing Drew had ever done.

Father, I'm lost here. I thought I was finally on the right track. Now everything almost seems worse than before.

Tomorrow he'd get to the bottom of the complaint and figure out how Jessica had drawn her false conclusion. Right now he had to make her listen to reason.

He found her squatting beside a bed of radishes, searching under the security lights for nonexistent weeds. An uncalculated gesture, he reached out to give her his hand for support. She slapped away his offering, and once again he felt the stirring of helplessness.

"Please let me do something for you, Jessica."

"Oh, right. I suppose you think a foot massage will fix this, too," she snapped.

It was his turn to snap back. "As a matter of fact, it might clean up your present disposition. And later I'll be happy to help you clean up your car and that mess you call home."

Continuing to resist the extended hand, she struggled to her feet and faced him. "That mess may not be my home much longer, thanks to you."

Drew shook his head, thoroughly confused. Clearly he was blowing it, so he dropped back and went in search of information.

"Exactly what did Ms. Chandler say?"

"That I'm in violation of the Sacred Arms homeowner's agreement. It seems there's a covenant against operating a business from my residence. Now I have thirty days to find *a place for everything* or face legal action by the association."

Drew turned away, searching his mind for an an-

swer. He needed to think this through, to make some
sense of what she was saying. Debating with her tonight, without the facts, would accomplish nothing.

When he faced her, she turned away dismissively.
He stepped forward and rested his palm lightly on her
shoulder. She stood, head bowed, staring down at the
rubber tip of her cane.

"Maybe this was someone's way of reminding you
that the natural beauty of Sacred Arms is what at-
tracted everyone to it. And maybe you owe it to the
other homeowners to respect and preserve that."

She lifted an amazed face to him.

"Drew, I *created* that natural beauty. This is *my
work.*" She emphasized the last two words by pointing toward her heart.

"Look around you," she insisted.

He did, admiring the host of colors in beds of lush
green, softened by the glow of the tall lamps.

"Most of what you see has been here less than
three years and it's the work of my own hands. The
ferns, the flowers, the vegetables, everything but the
trees and the oldest shrubs. And that's just because I
haven't had the time or the physical ability to get to
them yet. But I will." Her voice became a whisper.
"At least, I hope I will."

Jessica's face was in his shadow, but Drew knew
there was determination in those emerald eyes when
she turned to face him again.

"I love this place, Drew, just like everyone else.
But make no mistake, nobody knows better than I do

that its beauty wasn't nearly this 'natural' a few years ago."

He had to concede. "You're right, and I'm sorry for what I said. I'll clear this up tomorrow." He'd find a way to fix things.

She held up both palms, a sign to stop.

"The covenants are clear and my options are very limited. In thirty days if I can't afford a new place for Living Colors, I'm going to sell and go back to Texas with Becky Jo."

"No," he insisted. "We'll work this out with Ms. Chandler in the morning."

Jessica released a deep sigh and leaned tiredly on her cane as she stooped to pick up Frasier's leash. "Listen to me. You've done quite enough already. I don't need your help. Stay out of my business. And stay away from me."

Drew's stomach churned at the dismissive words. "I'm sorry you feel that way. I'd like to clear up this confusion, but I won't get involved if I'm not wanted."

He'd come home with such high hopes, and he suddenly felt helpless to unravel this misunderstanding. If he denied the claim, she wouldn't believe him. Not tonight, anyway.

"If you need help, anything at all, just call. Otherwise I'll do as you ask and stay away."

"That should make everybody happy." She turned and left him standing alone in the dark.

"Everybody but me," he whispered to himself.

* * *

Drew backed the truck into his usual parking space the next afternoon at Metro Muscle. Glancing to the right, he spotted the stack of mail resting where he'd tossed it the day before. He thumbed past several envelopes, pausing over a postcard from Peachtree Christian Church.

"'Please worship with us again,'" he read aloud, then flipped the card over to note the list of outreach services provided by the staff.

"That was quick." Hank poked his head into the open passenger window. "Thanks for making the lunch run for us."

Drew slid the card into his shirt pocket and turned toward his partner. "Think you can manage without me this afternoon?"

"No problem, but don't forget you have plans tonight with that guy who's flying in from Chicago. Since he's paying up front for a full restoration on his Boss, I think we should buy him a nice dinner in exchange for that check."

Drew thumped the steering wheel with the heel of his left hand. "That's right."

"You need me to take him off your hands?" Hank offered.

"I'd better handle it. I've been negotiating this deal with him for a week and I don't want to throw a wrench into his works now."

"If you're sure."

"I am. But I need to do something important before it gets any later. Would you mind?"

Hank grabbed the sack of burgers and fries off the seat and stepped back with a smart salute.

The church parking lot was nearly empty. Drew's eyes adjusted to the dim light as he stepped into the quiet vestibule. He followed the praise music that filtered through an open doorway.

"May I help you?"

Recognizing the pastor, Drew extended his hand.

"Good afternoon, sir. I'm Andrew Keegan. Am I interrupting?"

"Interruptions are often the best part of my day." The man smiled and gestured toward a chair. "I'm Joseph Driskell, the senior pastor."

"I know." Drew pulled the postcard from his pocket. "I attended a service here a couple of weekends ago."

"Great. We hope you'll join us for worship again. What brings you here today?"

Drew glanced down at the card in his hand. "I see you offer counseling services. Do I need an appointment?"

Pastor Driskell moved from behind his desk and took the chair next to Drew. "Why don't you tell me what's bothering you and then we'll decide about further counseling."

Drew's chest swelled with a deep breath. He twined his fingers together and leaned forward with his elbows on his knees.

All the practiced thoughts fled as he blurted, "I'm

letting everybody down, and I'm afraid God's at the top of the list.''

''How are you letting everyone down?''

''My father expects me to follow through with our plan for my career, but I can't. Everything was all mapped out until I met Jessica and now nothing's going the way I'd anticipated.''

The pastor smiled. ''In the thirty-two years I've been in ministry, I've found very few lives that unfolded according to our expectations. God has a way of changing our plans, and we never see it coming. But the great thing about God is that He'll never give you more change than you can handle.''

''It's my father who can't handle it.''

Pastor Driskell leaned back and crossed his arms. He squinted behind his horn-rimmed glasses as if to get a better look at Drew.

''Are you the oldest child in your family?''

''As a matter of fact, I am.''

''What kind of relationship do you have with your father?''

''We're close.'' Drew dropped his head and stared at his hands. ''As long as he's calling the shots.''

The older man leaned in, laying a warm palm on Drew's forearm.

''And you think by letting your father down you're letting God down, too?''

Drew nodded.

''I've seen this a thousand times. It's only natural that your image of our heavenly Father would be colored by your experience with your earthly father. If your father always has to have the last word it only stands to reason that God the Father would, too, right?''

Drew agreed by giving the pastor a weak smile.

''But God doesn't call the shots, Andrew. He gives us free will to make our own decisions. We experience rewards or suffer consequences because of those decisions, but either way He still loves us. When we consciously live in His will that's when all things can work together according to His purposes.''

As Drew considered the wisdom of the pastor's words, his own worries fled and he thought of Jessica. ''I have a friend who was abandoned by her father. She doesn't think God's there for her. He's too busy to answer her prayers.'' Drew looked for confirmation.

''Exactly.'' The pastor nodded. ''Lots of people come to the same conclusion. It's understandable these days when so few parent-child relationships are based on unconditional love and forgiveness. But God is not limited by human characteristics or failings. He doesn't view us through human eyes. He sees His children cleansed by the perfect sacrifice of Christ.''

''That's a lot to think about,'' Drew conceded.

''It always has been.'' Pastor Driskell chuckled, his warm gray eyes crinkled in a permanent pattern. ''Feel any better?''

''I'm not sure I can until my father is able to accept the new direction my life is taking.''

"Then I'll pray that in God's perfect timing your father's heart will be softened to your decision."

"Thank you, sir." Drew stood and extended his hand. "May I come back to visit with you again?"

"Absolutely. Will you be here on Sunday for worship?"

"I'm certain of it," Drew answered.

"Will your friend come with you?"

"Good question. That's an area where I'm not certain of anything."

At midnight Sacred Arms was dark and quiet. Drew closed and locked the garage door. To stretch his legs after a long evening of sitting with a client, he walked the fieldstone path around the far side of his building.

A soft light glowing through the shuttered windows of the Commons recreation hall caught his attention. Figuring a neighbor was cleaning up after a private event, he turned toward the copper-domed structure. The heavy door swung open easily, admitting him into the cool, silent hallway.

"Hello?"

His hesitant greeting bounced off the marble floor and echoed against the tall ceiling. Getting no response, he continued toward the source of the light that slipped from a door ajar at the end of the corridor. He stood quietly outside the door listening for activity. There was no sound at all, but he had an innate sense that someone was in the room.

Once again he cautiously offered a "Hello?" and

slowly pushed the door wide. The single word was all he could manage as he caught sight of the living rainbow contained by the four walls.

Color was everywhere! Crates and crates of flowers, ready to be planted. Petals of brilliant blue, shocking pink, eye-popping orange and buttery yellow softly stirred under the slight wind from an overhead fan. Healthy green ferns, waxed and shining, waited to be coupled with the colorful blooms and repositioned into the new pots, each one an individual work of art.

The assembly line was set up on makeshift worktables of plywood atop sturdy sawhorses. There was every stage of creation, from the skid of somehow familiar empty pots to the rows of finished arrangements.

He moved to get a closer look at the containerized gardens that were complete, down to the shiny silk ribbons adorned with golden lace.

As he reached to inspect the delicate handiwork, the rustle of movement in a dark corner caught his attention. Without a sound he turned slowly in the direction of the motion. A sympathetic smile slid across his lips as he saw the form asleep on the floor.

Jessica lay with her back to him, curled in a ball beneath a ragged old quilt, her blond head resting on a sack of Spanish moss. The covering rose and fell slightly as she breathed deeply, lost in heavy sleep. On the floor beside her an alarm clock ticked away the minutes, probably only a few hours from shattering the silence.

Unable to resist the tangle of softness that spread across the unlikely pillow, he silently crossed the floor and squatted beside her. With no one to see, he gently brushed the back of his hand down the length of Jessica's hair. Careful not to disturb her sleep, he coiled silky strands around his fingers, releasing her unique scent.

Shampoo and potting soil.

Jessica chose that moment to roll over and shift to her other side. Just for a second her heavy lids opened and she smiled dreamily. He held his breath, wanting to reach out and touch her, to make her know he was real. Her lids slid closed again and she dropped back to sleep with a drowsy moan.

The soft sound was almost his undoing. The choice between leaving her to rest for the few hours remaining and waking her to steal those hours for himself was a battle.

Until he recalled that she didn't trust him.

"Stay away from me." Her words rang in his memory.

He considered the long conversation he'd had with Pastor Driskell. It stood to reason that Jessica's inability to rely on her father, the most important man in her life, would cause her to be suspicious of all men. Drew was no longer angry that she'd accused him, simply hurt.

No matter how drawn he was to the gorgeous creature under the faded quilt, he'd never impose himself where he wasn't wanted.

Standing, he backed away slowly, careful not to disturb anything in the room. Glad for the chance to slip out completely unnoticed and determined to do something to make things right.

Chapter Twelve

Three more days. Jessica glanced at the clock that had become her nemesis. Seventy-two hours. If she hadn't needed to keep such a close eye on the remaining time, she'd have hurled the ticking monster against the stone fireplace that took up a full wall of the cluttered recreation room.

If Madeline called one more time for a "minor request," Jessica was certain she'd scream.

The woman must think I'm a magician! she thought.

Could Jessica do something extra on the front steps? Would it be too much trouble to coordinate with the florist on the ribbon? Were there any edible flowers in season? Would she be free to spend the wedding day at the house organizing all the outdoor decorating?

There just weren't enough hours left to do everything, and the tick, tick, tick of the infernal clock reverberated in the room like a time bomb. Even making the short walk from the Commons to her own place was a luxury she'd all but given up days ago. Other than a quick trip each morning for a shower and clean clothes, she confined herself to the rec room.

Left alone to create the spectacular containerized gardens, Jessica was making her visions become reality one by one. Everywhere she turned, the living flowers were like her children. Their faces lifted for her approval and nodded their delicate heads in agreement.

Madeline had pushed far beyond the original plan. During the meal, two hundred vivid daylilies would cradle servings of spicy shrimp salad. There would be pleasing formations on the front steps that hinted of the bursts of color in the back garden. The same satin-and-lace ribbon would segue beautifully from the floral arrangements in the pre–Civil War chapel to the last pot of flowers by the back gate.

Flowers and ribbons were the least of Jessica's worries. The last request would be the hardest to fill and what she lacked, most of all, was time. Now she frantically called Sam Harrelson in search of a crew to support her with some expensive Saturday overtime.

"Oh, Sam, thank you so much!" She almost cried from relief. "If you can have two or three guys and a box truck here that morning, I swear I'll kiss you the next time I see you!''

The seventysomething great-grandfather would likely try to collect on the offer. ''Miss Holliday, don't you worry none. Me and my boys'll be over there at first light.''

Dressed in pedal pushers and what looked like an original Woodstock T-shirt, Becky Jo arrived with thick homemade sandwiches, a jug of sun tea and a worn-out pair of gardening gloves.

''I thought you had clients this afternoon.'' Jessica was suspicious, but grateful for the unexpected company.

''I did, but they all canceled on me. Weirdest thing.''

Jessica accepted the tall glass of tea and took a cool swallow to clear the lump suddenly lodged in her throat.

''You don't have to do this.''

''Yes, I do,'' Becky Jo replied. ''You can't afford to pay for help and you're too hardheaded to ask for it. I won't stand by and let you fail when this place and your business mean so much to you. You know I'd love to have you come back to Dallas with me. But only out of choice, not necessity.''

''Thank you,'' she whispered to her best friend. Jessica was enveloped in Becky Jo's hug.

''Goodness gracious. It looks like a rainbow exploded in here.'' The petite woman in the doorway was barely recognizable in rolled-up jeans, a denim work shirt and a baseball cap. If the voice hadn't given her away, the sparkling diamonds at her ears, neck and wrists would have done the trick.

"Valentine! What are you doing here and what in the world have you got on?" In the years since Jessica had purchased her home, she'd never seen Valentine Chandler in anything less than sheer nylons and alligator pumps.

"Well, dahhhlin', I thought you might be able to use a little help. Believe it or not, I'm not always in designer suits. As you can see, I do own one pair of jeans."

"Then let's get to work." Jessica beamed her approval.

Four hours later, Jessica was giving serious consideration to discharging her volunteer army. As much as she normally enjoyed the company of Becky Jo and Valentine, their constant barrage of good-natured insults was testing what little religion Jessica had.

"I told you to let me do the ribbons. I was tying gorgeous Christmas bows before you ever learned to tie shoes," Valentine complained to Becky Jo.

"You mean before *my mama* learned to tie shoes, don't you?" Becky Jo couldn't resist. "And besides, you're the one who insisted your years of haute couture were the perfect experience for picking just the right flowers for each pot, dahhhlin'."

"Well," Valentine huffed. "We could hardly trust your taste. For heaven's sake, you look like a two-pound bag of melted skittles half the time and a garage-sale junkie the other half.''

''Why, thank you, Valentine.'' Becky Jo smiled down at today's fashion statement. ''I never thought you really appreciated my multidecade retro look. Actually, I wasn't sure you could see it for the glare off all that cubic zirconia.''

Valentine held out a hand and cast an approving smile at her jewels. ''You better hope you have to shade your eyes from stones like these one day, dahhhlin' girl. And you could, if you'd just let me take you shopping someplace besides the thrift shop.''

Jessica listened silently, her agitation mounting as the two women exchanged fashion tips veiled as insults. To make matters worse, everything coming off the assembly line looked, well, nothing at all like the pieces she had crafted by herself.

The personal touch she'd worked so hard to achieve was simply not evident in the eight containerized gardens the team had put together. Nothing short of ripping them apart and replanting would be acceptable.

The clock ticked feverishly.

Sixty-eight hours left and I might as well have spent the last four in a bubble bath, for all the work I've accomplished, she thought.

A quick count indicated that there were still two dozen planters to be etched with metallic gold and decorated with the now dwindling supply of expensive ribbon. Then came the creative part of combining the many blossoms to produce a garden that was similar to the rest, but uniquely different.

Jessica had busied herself with the pots, glad to delegate the planting to Becky Jo and Valentine for a few hours. Big mistake. They were good friends who meant well, but they were also friends who would drive her out of business if she didn't get rid of them fast.

"Hey, ladies. Can a guy crash this private party?"

The question bounced off the high ceiling. All three women turned toward the masculine voice.

"There you are, you handsome rascal!" Valentine's immediate gushing over Drew Keegan made Jessica and Becky Jo exchange puzzled looks, eyebrows raised in question. Valentine held out her arms for a hug. "I haven't seen you in a coon's age."

It was evident he'd come to understand hugging was a standard Southern greeting. Without pause, Drew returned the embrace. Above Valentine's head he nodded hello to the other two women, then turned his head to survey the room.

"Wow, Jessica, you've done some amazing work here."

She cut her eyes at him skeptically.

"I mean it." He nodded approval. "It's stunning."

"Thank you. It's nice to get credit for one's hard work now and then." She impaled him with an icy stare.

"What have you been doing with yourself?" Valentine came to his rescue.

"I've been on the road quite a bit lately, scouting the countryside for special parts and partial restorations we can complete for our showroom."

"Well, the folks at Sacred Arms miss you." Valentine spoke pointedly at Jessica. "So don't stay away so long."

Jessica turned her back to the group, determined to ignore his presence.

Her dismissal didn't seem to affect Drew. "Actually I'm home for the next week and looking forward to some time to hide in my own closet, if I want to."

Jessica sputtered into the glass of tea she'd just raised to her lips. Embarrassed, she glanced around to see two heads turned in concern, a third in amusement. She waved over her shoulder to show she was okay.

He clapped his hands together and rubbed them in anticipation. "Jessica introduced me to a place that serves great Mexican food. Would you ladies consider accepting a dinner invitation?"

Jessica remained with her back to the others, eyes fixed on her work. By now she figured the three would get her silent message. She should have known better.

"Heck, yeah, if you really mean it," Becky Jo agreed.

That did it. Jessica whipped around to take in the scene of her roommate making a date with their traitorous neighbor.

"As a rule, I don't go out during the week, but a

girl does have to eat.'' Valentine cast in her lot with the others.

All three turned hopefully toward Jessica, who shook her head emphatically. She should be grateful to him for getting the two out of her hair. Instead she felt her stomach rumble with jealousy.

''I couldn't possibly leave.'' When she noticed her friends' guilty faces she immediately added, ''But you two go on. You've earned it for all the help you've given me today. I'm so far ahead now that I can get a good night's sleep.''

''How about some carryout?'' Becky Jo offered.

''That would be great.''

''Do you need anything else?'' Drew asked. ''Some of those pots look pretty heavy. If they have to go up on that table just let me know and I'll be glad to lift them for you.''

For the first time she let herself stare him directly in the eye. He stood there so appealing, so innocent. It was unnerving and he knew it. He was doing it on purpose, complimenting her work, offering dinner, wanting to help.

''Thanks, but I have everything under control.''

She remembered the clock.

I hope.

Dinner was lively and enlightening. Drew nursed sweet tea and the two women expertly squirted lime into their long-neck bottles, regaling their host with stories of growing up in the South. Their formative years were decades apart, but they were sisters under the skin, with amazingly similar stories of Easter shoes and beauty pageants.

With three empty bottles to her credit, Becky Jo couldn't resist asking Drew why he'd complained about Jessica's business. Before he could defend himself, Valentine's head popped up from the earnest effort of folding a fajita.

"Is that what Jessica thought? That Drew was the one who complained?"

"Yes," the other two chorused.

Valentine pressed a palm to her flushed brow.

"Mercy sakes alive! I didn't tell her it was our property developer, Daniel Ellis, who called because I knew she'd be mortified to think he was critical of her. They've always been so fond of each other and, quite frankly, I was surprised he did such a thing."

Becky Jo took another sip and nodded in thought.

"That's more like it. I was pretty sure Drew wouldn't do a dirty thing like that." She stared him down. "But then you haven't burned me like you have Jess."

Drew turned in his chair to get a better view of the bountiful woman beside him.

"You want to explain that comment? How have I burned Jessica?"

"For starters, there was that ambush down at your garage. Too bad, because I really liked the old guy till he helped you set Jess up."

"We did not set her up."

"Did you take her for a ride, buy her ice cream, kiss her and then tell her to clean up her business practices?"

"Yes, but I didn't mean to insult Jessica. I was giving helpful suggestions."

"Looked more like a tactical maneuver to her. In other words, you set her up."

He appealed to Valentine for support. She gave a "no dice" shake of her platinum head. Guilt inched up his back as he faced reality. Jessica had seen right through his careful "plan."

Becky Jo popped a chip piled high with salsa into her mouth and chewed thoughtfully.

"You were with her on one of the toughest nights of her life when she visited the ADT for the first time after her accident. You didn't warn her about your long lost love, who just happens to be the Wicked Witch of the South. Then you left her to entertain your sister while you and Amelia smooched it up in the aisle, right?"

"Well, that's an abridged version of what happened." Guilt stopped inching and shot straight through him at the scene she must have endured. "I had no idea Jessica saw us."

He steeled himself for the story about Jessica hiding in his closet. When they only continued to give him the evil eye he silently thanked her for keeping it quiet.

Drew mumbled his thoughts. "When you put things in her perspective, I guess it's not so hard to understand why she jumped to the conclusion I let her down. Again.''

''Jessica's father was a five-star jerk when it came to living up to his word,'' Becky Jo confided. ''She doesn't trust men easily, especially if they come complete with a uniform.''

Becky Jo's words echoed those of Pastor Driskell.

''And I've been confirming what she believes about men.'' Drew stated the fact.

''So what are you going to do about it now, dahhhlin'?'' Valentine hiccuped.

''Yeah, Rambo, what's your next move?''

''I'm going to give you girls a ride home and then give our friend a hand. That is, if she'll let me.''

The thick beef burritos were still warm when Drew set the carryout sack on the plywood tabletop. They'd make a hearty breakfast when she woke up.

Jessica was already covered by the patchwork quilt. Earlier he'd noted the tired slump to her shoulders. There were dark circles under the emerald eyes and her dancer's posture was bent with fatigue. She slept soundly now, one hand clutching the cover to her chin, the other a resting place for her cheek.

Once again he studied the room appreciatively, but noted also how much work was left to do. There was even more dirt on the floor than before, a sign of the frantic activity that had been taking place. He counted the number of completed gardens and then the remaining empty pots. She was definitely on the back side of her mission.

For Jessica's sake, he was thankful the wedding would be over in a few days so she could rest in her own bed. He glanced again at the completely exhausted form under the frayed covering. His heart flip-flopped in sympathy. An invisible fist reached right into his chest and squeezed hard.

Lord, I want so much to obey Your will for my life. I've disappointed my father and upset the entire Crockett family, but I believe You've led me to this moment. My heart is so full of warmth when I'm near Jessica. Please demonstrate to her that she can trust Your guidance as much as I do.

Drew noted a few ways he could get away with helping on the spot. He'd trust God to show him the rest later.

Drawing upon years of stealth training, Drew moved about the room like a phantom, never making a sound. He braced the middle of her worktable more securely and lifted the heavy pots, careful to position them just as she'd arranged the others.

It took great restraint, but he resisted the desire to organize all her blooms and sweep up the loose potting soil. Before calling it a night, he paused curiously over her long "to do" list, rubbed his palms together at a crossed-off notation and slipped away.

When the alarm clock shrilled at 5:00 a.m., Jessica rolled over on the hard floor and groaned. Her never-ending list of chores seemed insurmountable on four hours of sleep.

Years of self-discipline kicked in, and within fifteen minutes she was at it again. She stood at her worktable, gently rotating her painful shoulders and twisting side to side to eliminate the night's stiffness. Becky Jo would be along shortly with a thermos of strong hot coffee. Meanwhile, Jessica dug in to the fragrant carryout sack and groaned with pleasure at the first mouthful of tender beef and refried beans.

As she chewed, grateful for the unusual breakfast, she noticed minor changes in the room. The heaviest pots waited on the makeshift table, positioned perfectly for painting to begin. She smiled as she finished the tortilla. Of course. Becky Jo must have come back last night and set up for today's work. Jessica made a mental note to thank her friend, used a broken screwdriver to pop open a fresh can of gold paint and got to work.

"Caffeine, anyone?" Becky Jo stood in the doorway, holding a thermos and a steaming mug of coffee.

"Thanks for the help with the heavy stuff." Jessica accepted the mug with one hand and motioned toward the workbench.

"What do you mean?"

"You didn't do this when you brought the food last night?" Jessica's insides began to squirm.

"Heck, no. Drew offered to bring it over."

Jessica took in the scene again. The heavy work that would have stressed her knee was done. Her gut twisted anxiously and she didn't even consider blaming it on the burrito. Then things got more complicated.

Becky Jo's face lit up. "Oh, I haven't told you yet! Valentine said Daniel Ellis was the person who complained about Living Colors. Didn't Drew tell you?"

"No, I never even knew he was here."

She flinched at the idea of herself asleep on the floor, mouth hanging open and drool on her cheek. Becky Jo's last comment saved her from dwelling on the disgusting picture.

"What's this about Daniel Ellis?" Jessica asked.

The dinner conversation was replayed. When her friend finished with a smile, Jessica knew Becky Jo was pleased her instincts about their neighbor had been correct.

"So why would Ellis do that if you're friends?"

Jessica scratched her head. "I don't know. I'll have to work on that when I don't have to worry about so much else."

The memory of how she'd treated Drew surfaced. Jessica hid her eyes behind both hands.

Oh, God, show me how to make this right, she silently pleaded.

Recalling Drew's face when she'd slapped his outstretched hand and told him to stay away, she grimaced. "I am such a creep! I can't believe he's still speaking to me."

"Much less trying to help you."

"Oh, thanks."

"Don't mention it."

"Well, that's something else I'll have to work out after this weekend." If not for the sand streaming through her imaginary hourglass, she would have dealt with it right away. Jessica sighed heavily, wondering if she'd ever find the right words to apologize for misjudging him so badly.

Becky Jo checked her watch and headed for the door. "You gonna be okay here today?"

Time to snap out of it. "Sure, and thanks again for your help yesterday. I wouldn't be this far along without you."

The short woman cast her gaze astutely around the room. No trace of the arrangements she and Valentine had produced remained. Instead, everything once again had Jessica Holliday's special touch.

Becky Jo smiled wryly. "Yeah, right. You'd be another day ahead if not for all our help. Well, don't worry. I have a full schedule today and Valentine's getting her hair done. So if you need anything, call Metro Muscle." She smiled as she turned to leave.

"What about Frasier?" Jessica suddenly remembered to ask.

"I'm on my way to drop him off at the groomer. Probably won't ever want to come home, the ungrateful mutt."

The heavy door fell closed and Jessica was alone. She leaned elbows on plywood and thought about Drew. Obedient son, doting brother, practical businessman, understanding friend, trusting Christian. The man would be an incredible partner.

The wriggling in her stomach became a fluttering in her chest. She picked up her paintbrush and went back to work with a fresh load of determined hope and fifty-six hours till the couple said, "I do."

Chapter Thirteen

Jessica woke in her own bed after sleeping like the dead. She'd done it! Ten hours till the wedding and everything was on schedule. She'd managed to fill all of Madeline's special requests, with only one exception. And that was so outrageous that no one could be expected to take it seriously. Butterflies, for goodness sake!

She pulled on yesterday's clothes, knowing she'd allowed time to shower and dress before the wedding. Needing one last check on everything, just to calm the pounding of her heart, she opened the security door and stepped out into the early light of the still-quiet morning.

Nestled in the rec room, her magnificent work waited to be unveiled. Pots of azure monkshood, brilliant stargazer lilies and scarlet pelargoniums were poised to become the splashes of color in an otherwise monochromatic garden. Large urns, planted with classic topiary, would provide formal symmetry to the informal patios. Each piece was as heavy as it was splendid. Jessica was grateful for the muscular arms and strong backs that would position the container gardens.

Returning by the front pathway, she noticed a large note taped to the outside door. The scrawling message instantly ruined her morning.

"Miss Holliday, we think Daddy had a stroke last night. He'll be okay, but Mama and us boys are at the hospital with him today. He asked me to come tell you he was sorry to let you down. I'm sorry, too. Sam's boy, Noble."

Jessica stared numbly at the paper. "Poor Sam," she said aloud as she read the note two more times, absorbing the impact of the words. The covered truck she needed to get the flowers safely to the reception site wasn't coming. Neither were the men who would lift and carry the arrangements she'd poured her heart into for the past week.

The fit of emotions that threatened would have to wait. She hurried toward her home, clutching the bad news and fighting down panic.

"Beej!" Jessica began to call the moment the door sprang open. On the third shout, her friend's groggy face appeared around the doorway as Becky Jo hurried down the stairs.

"What is it? Who's dead?"

"I might as well be." Jessica handed over the note.

''Oh, no, Jess.'' Becky Jo stared down at the message. ''Who else can we call?''

Jessica shook her head. ''On this short notice? Nobody I can afford.''

''Go ask Drew. He's got that big truck and more muscles than the law allows. And he's offered to help.''

''After what I did? No way!'' Jessica threw her palms up and backed away from the suggestion.

''Calm down and listen to me.'' Becky Jo caught Jessica by the hand, hauling her over to the sofa.

''This is no time to be stubborn. Your future depends on how things go today. You don't have *time* for pride. So don't look a handsome gift horse in the mouth.''

Becky Jo always had been able to read Jessica like a book. Her friend had caught the guilt vibes she radiated

''Look, Jessica, he made mistakes. You made mistakes. We all make mistakes. He's a control freak and he wants to help. Make his day.''

Jessica studied the toes of her ancient sneakers. What choice did she have when it came right down to it? She'd worked her fingers to the bone on this job and if she had to go begging for help, so be it.

How hard could it be?

Besides, she wouldn't see him again after the wedding, anyway. Amelia would see to that.

The decision made, Jessica stood. ''Okay. You're right.''

She squared her shoulders, focusing as if she were about to step onto the stage for the biggest performance of her life. With her hand on the doorknob, she turned back and raised crossed fingers. Becky Jo did the same and then shooed her with both hands.

As Jessica raised her fist to knock on Drew's door, she noted the time. Seven o'clock. Nine hours to go. She rapped sharply and waited. A shadow blocked the peephole.

"He's here! Thank You, Lord," she whispered.

The door opened an inch, but Jessica didn't see anyone through the crack. Then movement below eye level caught her attention and she looked down to see Amelia.

"What do you want?"

Jessica was mortified. Begging was going to be much harder than she thought. "I need to speak to Drew."

"Well, he's in the shower."

The thought of Amelia with Drew pushed Jessica closer to tears. She swallowed her hurt feelings and remaining pride. Being humble was highly overrated.

"I'll just wait next door. Will you tell him it's an emergency? Please?"

The door closed in her face. She heard the dead bolt and wondered if her message would get delivered. There was no choice but to wait at home and find out.

* * *

Drew heard the front door close as he walked out onto the landing, completely dressed, hair still damp from his shower. He watched as Amelia sprinted back into the kitchen and continued to pull breakfast pastries from a white bakery carton.

She fidgeted with the doughnuts. "Would you like breakfast while we talk?"

"No, thanks." He took the mug she offered, but waved away the starchy sweets. "It's too bad you didn't call first. I could have saved you a trip, because I'm on a tight schedule today."

"You're right, of course. I shouldn't have shown up like this," she conceded. "But I still think we can work things out, Drew."

He ushered her toward the door, put her pocketbook in her hands, grabbed his own keys and locked up behind them. He helped Amelia into her convertible and stepped away. "There is nothing to work out. There never was."

Jessica's breath caught in her throat when she heard the rumble of Drew's car. She snatched up her cane and reached the parking lot just as he was pulling away. She hurried out into the middle of the driveway, waving furiously to get his attention above the thundering engine.

"Drew!" She waved frantically. "Drew!"

He never slowed as he passed under the ornamental archway. She leaned forward, her hands on her knees, unable to bear the weight of the moment. The tears sprang from deep inside, rushing hard, choking her with their force.

Oh, God, please do something. I can't handle this alone anymore, she begged.

Her lungs burned and she pushed upright to take in oxygen. Through her tears she saw a blur of red brake lights and Drew Keegan running toward her.

He caught Jessica to his chest, muscular arms wrapped protectively around her.

She'd never felt such relief in her life. Suddenly there was a sense of completeness where there had been a huge void. When she lifted her eyes, she knew they were shamelessly full of apology and need. She could only stare through the tears that would not stop.

He pulled a fresh bandanna from his pocket, wiped her face and planted a tender kiss on her forehead.

"What on earth is wrong?"

"The wedding is less than nine hours away, my work crew just canceled and I can't even begin to tell you what's at stake today. I know I don't deserve it, but if you'll help me, Drew, I promise I'll explain everything tomorrow."

He smiled, dimple and all, and guided her to the sidewalk.

"Let me make a couple of phone calls. I'll meet you in the Commons in five minutes." He ran his hand down the back of her hair as she turned to walk away.

A glance over her shoulder sent a thrill of hope

through her heart. He was still watching, tenderness etched in his features.

"I'm so sorry," she said quietly.

"Me, too."

Spilling over with a riot of blossoms, the last mosaic planter took its place in Madeline Shure's backyard. The result of Jessica's planning was spectacular. A stately yard of boxwoods was transformed into a field of living color.

"You did it!"

Drew was close. She could feel the heat radiating from his chest. She turned to face him.

"I hope you know how grateful I am for all your help."

"I can see that." He smoothed runaway blond strands out of her face. "But really, I don't deserve much credit. I just did the heavy work."

"But if you hadn't—"

He touched the tips of his fingers to her lips, silencing her. She rested her hand on the back of his, inhaling his scent, wanting so much to kiss the fingertips.

She pulled his hand away. "Please, let me thank you. You tried to be a good friend and I misjudged you terribly."

"That's an apology, not a thank-you. And I have apologies to make myself, so why don't we do them justice later?"

She nodded her agreement.

His eyes widened at his watch. "I have a very important errand to run and it can't wait much longer."

"Oh, sure." She stepped back, suddenly conscious of their closeness. "I've already taken up enough of your day."

"No, that's not what I meant at all. My time is your time. I just have to take care of an important detail and then I'm all yours again."

She cocked her head, puzzled.

"I mean, would you mind if I come with you tonight, just in case you need me for any last-minute heavy work?" he explained.

"I can't imagine that would be necessary. And don't you have plans of your own?"

"I've cleared my calendar just for you. Permanently." His brown eyes bored into hers.

"Well, if you don't mind doing me another favor."

Drew reached for her hand. "It's not a favor. I want to be here." He gave it a soft squeeze. "I'll be dressed and back here before the wedding party returns from the church. Are you going to the ceremony?"

"I think so. I'd really like to see how everyone reacts to the decorations. If they're as favorable as we expect, the wedding coordinator wants me to work on another project with her next month."

Her heart melted when his eyes lit up at the news.

"That's great, Jess." He spoke the shortened version of her name softly, like an endearment. "I'll be here waiting when you get to the reception."

* * *

Jessica almost cried when the couple kissed tenderly at the altar. And she choked up again when the guests mounted the steps of the Shure home, exclaiming over what was only the beginning of the magical mosaic gardens.

But the tears spilled unchecked when she spotted Captain Andrew Keegan, more handsome than ever in his dark suit and crisp white shirt. He stood near the topiary flanking the table that held a six-tiered wedding cake.

She waved a brief greeting through the crowd, then detoured to the powder room to repair her mascara and to give herself a pep talk.

"No more tears, Jessica Holliday! You've done it! Now go out there and enjoy the party." She pointed emphatically toward her image in the mirror. "And don't read too much into his being here."

She tilted her head toward the ceiling, closed her eyes and clasped hands beneath her chin. *Forgive me, Father. I'm beginning to understand that I am blessed. I wouldn't be where I am this moment without You and the help of my friends. Thank You.*

Passing through the hallway, Jessica accepted a frosty glass of club soda from a passing waiter. She eased through the crowd, careful not to trip anyone with her cane. Stepping outside through double doors, she listened to the chatter of guests, overhearing praise for the extraordinary wedding and reception.

Catching her eye, Drew inched his way through the crowd to where she stood.

"Hello" was all she dared.

His even white teeth flashed beneath the Rhett Butler mustache, and both cheeks dimpled his delight at seeing her. Jessica took his extended hand. He held her at arm's length, turning her once, slowly. She hoped he appreciated her upswept hair and the clingy appeal of the satin gown.

"You're breathtaking."

"Thank you." She sighed.

"And, of course, you know these two," the mother of the bride said by way of introduction before she moved on to her other guests.

Both heads turned to find Amelia walking toward them. Breaking social protocol by wearing white to a wedding, she was pure chic in her size-two ivory suit.

"Surprise."

"Yes, it is," Drew agreed. "I wasn't expecting you to be here."

"I just couldn't think of an excuse to decline Madeline's invitation. Jessica, be a dear and get me a glass of champagne."

Drew stiffened. "She'll do nothing of the kind. Jessica's a guest, too."

"Oh, sorry." Amelia's attempt to sound sincere was weak. "Madeline *is* paying Jessica to be here today. I presumed she was working."

"She'd hardly be wearing that beautiful gown if she were working."

Amelia looked Jessica over critically. "Yes, it's nice. I thought so the last time I saw her wear it, too."

"If you'll excuse me." Jessica turned to leave.

"Oh, no, you don't." Drew caught her by the elbow and pulled her to his side. "You're a vision in that gown and I'm not letting you out of my sight this evening."

There was the slightest gasp from Amelia before she stomped into the crowd.

Two hours into the reception the bride's father invited everyone to the terrace for the cutting of the wedding cake. Along with two hundred of the Shures' closest friends, Jessica slowly made her way toward the bride's table. Once again she spotted Drew standing where she'd first found him, near the pots of topiary.

He was alone and motioning her to join him just behind the wedding cake. As she moved closer, she noticed something unusual. One of her tall ficus arrangements had been enclosed from the bottom up in a silky gold bag tied at the top with fine golden thread. It was barely more than an opaque mist concealing the plants inside.

When she stood beside him, he handed her the end of the thread and whispered softly, "As the bride cuts the cake, give this a pull and step away." Before she could question him, he faded into the crowd.

The newlyweds took their positions, placed hands together on the silver cake knife and cut into the bottom tier. As instructed, Jessica gave a tug and moved to one side. The crowd fell silent as the golden bag dropped into a shimmering puddle around the planter and the soft shapes inside began to move, fluttering to life, floating into the air.

At the collective "Ohhh" of their guests, the bride and groom turned toward a living kaleidoscope as hundreds of butterflies stirred from their rest to take flight in dazzling splendor.

The photographer's flash popped again and again, catching the incredible sight of the bridal gown now decorated with tiger swallowtails and mourning cloaks, a single huge monarch perched atop the groom's shoulder.

Equally amazed, Jessica was awed by the sight.

The bride and groom turned in her direction and raised their glasses as their guests did the same.

"No... I didn't... You don't understand." She tried to explain.

"Just take the credit. You deserve it." Drew was at her side, arm around her waist, encouraging her to accept the accolades.

She lifted her gaze to him, not willing to take praise she hadn't earned. "But I didn't do anything."

"Make no mistake, no one knows better than I do this beauty wasn't nearly this 'natural' a few hours ago." He echoed the words she'd said to him in the darkness at Sacred Arms. "You did everything. Now take your bow."

Praying that her knee would hold, the former

dancer executed the same deep curtsy she'd practiced since she was a little girl back in Longview, Texas. The rush of pride and accomplishment in this garden was as strong as it had ever been in the footlights.

As she rose, Jessica felt the warmth of Drew's palm cupping her elbow. She tilted her head toward him, her eyes moist with emotion. His smile was possibly the sweetest sight she'd ever seen. Her heart thundered in her ears as he lowered his face and covered her trembling lips with his own.

Before a hundred pairs of wide eyes, Andrew pulled Jessica to his chest. As he held her possessively, she mirrored his actions. Twining her arms around his waist, she molded herself to the incredible man and melted into the emotion of the kiss.

A ripple of laughter brought her back to reality. Reluctantly she ended the kiss, silently praying there would be many more to come. She traced her fingertips along his jaw, resting them atop his lips. He kissed them softly, gave her a conspiratorial wink, turned her and gave her a light nudge toward the crowd.

Guests pressed close, surrounding her with congratulations and questions about her new business venture.

With his heart pounding from such a private moment acted out in public, Drew self-consciously accepted a slice of cake. He stepped to the edge of the patio, still within earshot of Jessica's accolades. His chest swelled more with each potential client who praised her handiwork and inquired about the unique planters. He noted that she frequently mentioned a business called Helping Hands. More than once she commented that God had led her to the unique place. There was no longer any doubt in Drew's mind. Jessica was beginning to recognize God's hand on her life.

Jessica seemed to be driving business to Helping Hands instead of grabbing the attention for herself. She was an amazing lady, and he felt so complete in her presence. How could he have been so wrong about God's plan for the right woman?

The *right* woman.

Jessica.

When he thought of her, his skin warmed and his heart raced. He would forever be stirred by the smell of potting soil and shampoo.

"Dear God, it's true. I love her," he whispered. "I love her and I don't even care that I got the plan all wrong. Pastor Driskell was right. You do have a way of changing our plans and giving us everything we need to deal with it."

As desperately as he wanted to share his heart and his faith with Jessica, he knew there was one other person who deserved to know first.

"Sir, are you still there? I said I love Jessica."

"I heard you the first time, son." Marcus sighed into the phone.

"I plan to ask her to be my wife. I wanted you and Faith to be the first to know. I was hoping for your blessing and Mom's diamond ring."

"Well, you won't get either of those things."

Drew imagined his father's face, distorted with disappointment.

"You're a grown man and I may not be able to stop you, but I sure won't help you. I don't know what this woman's hold is on you, but you're throwing your future away with this completely irresponsible decision."

Drew's head snapped back as if he'd been slapped by the angry words.

"This woman's *hold* on me is that she accepts me just as I am. Our future together won't ride on how much money I can make or what my title might be one day or how much influence I'll have. And you know what's even better than that, sir? She loves Faith the same way. Jessica treats her like a friend instead of a burden. And if Jessica will have me, our home will always be a place where my sister is welcome, whenever and for as long as she needs us."

The passion in his voice was obvious, but his father wasn't moved.

"Don't do this, Andrew. Give yourself some more time."

"Time to do what *you* expect? Isn't that what you mean, Father? All my life, even when it felt wrong for me, I followed your instructions. But this time I'm doing what I'm certain is right. I'm just sorry you can't share my joy.'' He paused, hoping his father would come to his senses and bless the union.

Drew spoke past the lump in his throat. ''Please give Faith a hug for me. Goodbye, sir.''

Chapter Fourteen

Jessica sat at her kitchen counter, Frasier at her feet, waiting for the knock that was sure to come at ten o'clock sharp. She smiled at the thought of something they finally had in common. Punctuality. Wasn't that the thing that was next to godliness? No, that was cleanliness. Never mind.

Ears still ringing with last night's compliments, she closed her eyes and whispered her gratitude, amazed how naturally prayer was becoming part of her life. Her faith was refreshed with each prayer. Next she enjoyed a mental replay of the evening. She'd thought such exhilaration from physical accomplishment was a thing of the past. It was a joyful revelation to know she'd been wrong. She'd been wrong about a lot of things, not the least of which was Andrew Keegan.

Three sharp blasts of a car horn opened her eyes. She hurried to the utility-room window and raised the blinds. She waved excitedly, motioned "just a minute," then headed for the front door, shouting up the stairs as she went.

"Beej! I'm gone!"

She bent to give Frasier's silky head a loving pat. "See ya later, buddy."

She reached for her shoulder bag, but her hand stopped short of the aluminum cane. Remembering last night's curtsy, she cautiously examined the knee for swelling below the red scar. Finding none, she flexed her leg back and forward several times, finally testing the strength of the knee with some careful pliés. With satisfaction, she left the cane in the umbrella stand and closed the door behind her.

"Wow! What a great surprise!" Clad in walking shorts and a bright yellow T-shirt, Jessica spread her arms to indicate the shining convertible.

Drew stood before her in faded jeans, holding open the passenger door. "I hoped you'd like it."

"I love it!" She beamed as she slipped into the seat.

And I love you, he thought to himself.

The realization had kept him up most of the night. Just knowing the woman he longed for was separated from him only by their common wall was almost too much to bear. He'd had visions of cutting a hole in that wall.

At 4:00 a.m. he'd finally given up the idea of sleep and opted for an early run to Metro. When the fluorescent overhead lights bounced off the red '68 convertible, he'd immediately thought of Jessica.

He slid in beside her and turned as he fastened the seat belt.

"I hope you don't mind what the wind does to that gorgeous hair." He allowed himself the bold pleasure of running his hand down the back of her honey-colored locks.

She smiled in response. Reaching into the pocket of the khaki shorts, she pulled out an elastic band.

"Not a problem."

He watched with fascination as she expertly worked the thick hair into a golden braid and snapped the elastic around its tail. Little wisps remained free around her face, bangs dancing in the morning breeze just above her eyelashes. He drank in the sight of her clean face, free of any pretentious makeup.

He couldn't help himself. He tugged the silky braid, gently urging her toward him. He smiled down into the emerald depths of her eyes, fighting to contain the joy in his heart. He wasn't sure of her feelings and hardly understood his own.

Jessica laid her hand on his arm. When she spoke, her voice was husky with emotion.

"As much as I value independence and wanted to do this on my own, you were the answer to a desperate prayer yesterday." He opened his mouth to speak, but she raised her palm, silencing him.

"I was wrong, Drew. I misconstrued something Valentine said and jumped to the conclusion you'd turned me in. I can't tell you how bad I feel about misjudging you, especially when I know how painful false judgment feels.''

She paused, searching his face. ''I'm sorry, Drew. Please forgive me.''

''Consider it forgiven and forgotten.'' He lightly brushed the back of his hand over her cheek and down along her jaw, his unspoken love growing at her mention of answered prayer.

Before he could pull away, Jessica caught his hand between her two, held it to her lips and kissed it sweetly. She looked surprised and slightly embarrassed at the impulsive act, before she released him and busied herself with the seat belt.

''What a perfect day for a drive,'' she said, tilting her face toward the warm sun.

He brought the vintage engine to life, studying her profile. Longing stirred as he admired the upturned face. He drew in a deep breath and eased the car into motion.

He planned to head north, toward the cooler temperatures of the Georgia mountains, but Jessica had another destination in mind. He gladly adopted her plan instead, following unfamiliar directions. Both were content to be silent, enjoying the wind on their skin and the quiet companionship.

The convertible slipped into a gravel parking lot with several dozen other cars. In no hurry to join the small crowd gathering for the art exhibit, they sat in the sunshine, eventually breaking the comfortable silence.

"Okay, confess," she insisted.

His eyebrows shot up in question. "Confess?"

"Don't play coy with me, mister. Where'd those butterflies come from and how'd you know about that in the first place?"

He tried to appear humble.

"I should probably start by apologizing for poking my nose into your business."

"You're forgiven." She made a forward motion with her hand. "Continue, please."

"Well, you probably figured out I played Santa's helper while you were asleep the other night."

She shielded her eyes with her hand. "Don't remind me. Seeing me passed out on the floor probably gave you nightmares."

"You were a Sleeping Beauty." He said it with all sincerity, then added with a smile, "And the loud snoring really helped cover any noise I made."

As her eyes widened, she punched him playfully in the arm. "That's probably the truth! Every roommate I ever had accused me of it."

"Anyway, I saw your list on the counter. I noticed that you'd checked off all the other stuff, but you'd crossed out the butterfly idea."

"It was one of Madeline's crazy requests, but I did make a small effort at it. I spoke to the manager of the butterfly house at Callaway Gardens to see if they'd sell them to me. She turned me down flat and

I had too much else to worry about at the time, so I just scratched it off the list.''

His voice was tinged with mischief. ''Well, I guess that's where being the son of Marcus Keegan can have its advantages. I did the same thing you did, but I tossed out my father's name a time or two. I assured her that he'd not only consider it a personal favor, but, along with replacing the stock, he'd agree to a scheduled visit during their next fund-raising campaign.''

Jessica covered her mouth to hold back the laughter. ''You didn't.''

''I did.'' He waved it off. ''Oh, he won't mind. He and Faith will come for a visit sooner or later, and he never tires of being a public servant. Anyway, after that it was just a matter of doing what you had written down. When you caught me just as I was leaving yesterday morning, that's where I was headed. All day long I was afraid I wouldn't get away from setting up in time to take care of that last detail.''

The smile left her face, replaced by true shock. Jessica seemed at a loss for words. She reached a trembling hand across the short distance that separated them and touched his bare forearm. Without hesitation he placed his own warm hand over hers, thankful he could caress her without guilt at last.

''You were going to do that for me even after the way I misjudged you?''

''Jess, you're not the only one who misjudged. I

said some really stupid things to you and my only
defense is selfish ignorance.''

Confused, she waited for him to explain.

''As hard as it may be to believe, outside of my
mother and Faith, I don't have a lot of experience
with women.''

Jessica snorted disgust and pulled away. He realized she was thinking of Amelia. He captured both of
her hands and turned her to face him.

''Hear me out, please.''

She stilled, staring intently into his eyes.

''Most of my adult life was spent in the military. I
went from one training environment to another and
very few of them included women. And even if they
did, most of my training involved dangerous endur-
ance situations. When the bottom line is literally survival, there's not much opportunity to develop inti-
mate relationships. At least, that's the way it was for
me. You have to be selfish on some level just to get
through each day.''

''But you're not a selfish person,'' she insisted.

''Thank you,'' he said. ''I like to think that's true.
But even in a situation where you're completely committed to a team, you are also responsible for yourself
and your own survival. The success of the mission
depends upon each person's desire to get into the target area, stay alive while you accomplish the goal and
get back out. As I said, it takes a certain amount of
selfishness to get you through it all.''

''But what did you mean about selfish ignorance?''

"Well, I'm certainly not proud of it, but I still get very focused on myself and my own survival. I tend to look at every situation in terms of how I can control the outcome. Unfortunately, I don't always take others into consideration when I do that and I make decisions ignorantly unaware of people's feelings. When my family calls me a control freak, it is *not* a compliment."

Jessica smiled tenderly at the revelation. "You are a bit of a control freak, but you're not selfish." She shook her head. "You're not, Andrew. A selfish man wouldn't spend time analyzing his own behavior and worrying how it affects the people who love him."

His pulse quickened at her mention of love.

"And I've noticed you occasionally lighten up a bit," she teased.

"It's not happening very fast," he admitted, "but I'm learning a little more each day that giving God dominion over my life means going with the flow and letting Him work things out."

Drew squeezed her fingers. "Jess, from the beginning I was so wrong about you. I expected you to conform automatically to my expectations so I could manage the outcome. That was terribly unfair and I don't blame you for misjudging me when I came on like Rambo."

"Let me ask you something," she said softly.

Still holding her hands in his, he nodded agreement.

"Why do you think you have to manage the outcome of things?"

"Because an uncontrolled outcome can mean failure. I understand what's expected of me and failure is never an option."

"Do you feel like your mission to get back with Amelia was a failure?"

"No," he said emphatically. "That plan was flawed from the outset, because it was *my* plan. It just took me a while to realize it. It may take longer, but I trust God to show me another way to reach my goals. He's going to do amazing things in my life."

"I envy your confidence. I want to learn to trust God like you do."

"I don't know any other way. I was a lot like you until a few years ago. I did everything on my own, fiercely independent, never completely relying on anyone else. And then one day I was so overwhelmed by the challenges in my life, I knew I wouldn't survive unless I let go and gave myself over to His will. It was the hardest thing I've ever done. And the smartest."

They were silent while she considered what he'd said.

"Would you mind if we get out of the car now?" she asked. "I'd like to stretch my legs and I have some people I want you to meet."

Sorry to see the intense honesty of the moment end, he shifted away and climbed out of the car.

Jessica met him as he came around the front fender

and surprised him by boldly reaching out and sliding her hands around his midsection. Standing tall and laying her cheek against his chest, she stilled as if listening to his erratic heartbeat.

His heart swelled with unspoken love as he enjoyed the wonder of having her embrace him for the first time. Several long moments later, she tilted her face up, a small smile on her lips and a shiny mist in her eyes.

"What do you say we go inside?" she suggested.

Jessica took the lead and Drew followed her down the path toward the Helping Hands Gallery.

As they waited patiently in line to enter the old barn, she explained.

"I met Gail Tinker at a craft warehouse. She was buying supplies for her students. I questioned one of the clerks about pottery paint. Gail overheard me, made a few suggestions and we struck up a conversation. I thought of her as soon as I got the Shure wedding contract."

"So she made all the pots you used for that project?"

"Not exactly. Gail's work is incredible and you'll see it in the gallery. But her students specialize in the mosaic pots."

The line moved. They left the bright sunshine behind, stepping into the gallery's shady entry. Jessica watched Drew's face as his eyes adjusted to the light. As expected, his interest soon changed from mild to intense.

The Sunday-afternoon class was in full swing. Students sat around low worktables, concentrating on their art. The unmistakably trusting eyes of Down's syndrome kids glowed with pride and achievement. In other faces Drew saw the childlike openness he loved in his baby sister.

Family members helped and cheered every accomplishment. Gail Tinker introduced her special students and then invited the guests into her gallery.

''This is where you brought Faith.'' A look of understanding dawned.

''That's right. I wondered if you'd ever made the connection between her pot and the ones I used for the wedding.''

He studied the students. ''All these people are…''

''Disabled.'' She finished his statement. ''In addition to her incredible talent as an artist, Gail has a degree in adult psychology. She specializes in working with the mentally challenged.''

''So this is a form of therapy?''

''In a way.'' She glanced at the whimsical surroundings.

The walls were covered with hand-painted fruit trees, heavy with fuzzy peaches and glistening apples. The barn's high ceiling was painted vibrant shades of sapphire, with dazzling comets and sparkling stars streaking across the pretend sky.

''Mostly Gail enjoys teaching them to be creative and independent. Designing the pots involves making their own choices. The result is something unique, entirely their own.''

Drew's misty eyes registered his approval.

"So they leave with a sense of accomplishment."

"Exactly." She nodded. "Just like Faith did."

Drew gestured toward the supply shelves. "Who pays for all this?"

"Until now, Gail funded it with the sales from her gallery. But with the economy slow, sales are down. She had to have some visibility, so I agreed to use her pots at the Shure wedding. Hopefully we'll draw attention and donations for Helping Hands."

Drew caught her waist and pulled her close, whispering into her hair, "Jessica Holliday, you're an incredible woman. You jeopardized your own success to help a friend."

She looked into the dark eyes. "It was for a very good cause. Everything I valued was already on the line, since I followed your advice and took that leap of faith."

"What do you mean?"

"I couldn't afford to pay for the plants up front, so I used my home as collateral."

"You risked your place at Sacred Arms on the project?" He sounded incredulous.

"I knew there was no risk involved. I was investing in myself, in my future. Now I know God really was in control."

"A prudent choice for a wise businesswoman." Drew pressed a kiss to her forehead. "Is there any chance you'd be willing to sell stock in your new venture?''

''We'll discuss taking my company public another time.'' She slipped reluctantly out of his embrace, shyly took his hand and led him toward the art exhibit.

Drew's sides literally ached from an evening of laughter. He couldn't remember another day in his adult life when he'd been so carefree.

The decision to end things with Amelia had been a weight off his shoulders. It simply wasn't ordained.

Too many years had passed. The high-spirited, demanding girl had grown into an arrogant woman. Her teenage vanity had become full-blown narcissism. And worse, Amelia had so little empathy for others. For her sake, he hoped that she didn't learn about compassion the hard way.

Learning the hard way. Boy, did he know about that.

Once he'd understood the value of experienced guidance, he'd followed it faithfully. The person he trusted most on earth was Marcus Keegan. Drew had never set a course in direct opposition to his father.

Until now.

Drew punched in the security code and held the door for Jessica.

''Could I interest you in a chocolate chip cookie?''

She shook her head, eyes sparkling under the soft overhead lights of the darkened hallway. ''After that delicious pasta, I couldn't. I actually lost a few pounds this past week, and now that I've made progress, I'm determined to stick with it. I'll never be a six again, but size ten might be nice.''

''Congratulations.'' He beamed approval. ''Let's celebrate with a diet cola.''

''Drew, it's really late, and I'm exhausted.'' She rested her hand on his chest. ''It's been a magical day.''

''Yes, it has,'' he whispered. ''And I'm not ready for the magic to end. Please stay with me for a while longer.''

Giving in, Jessica turned and crossed the threshold.

Track lights positioned above his sound system sprang to life at the flick of a switch, illuminating the collection of CDs. ''What would you like to hear?'' He bent to study the selection.

''You choose. I'll pour the soda.'' Jessica appeared right at home in the kitchen that was exactly like hers. Only neater. As she returned with two glasses, the room filled with soft music.

Taking Jessica by surprise, Drew grasped her by the waist and swept her into a perfect three-step turn. She expertly followed his lead even as a giggle bubbled to the surface. The drinks forgotten, he pulled her close and captured her mouth. She wrapped her arms around his neck and dumped ice-cold soda down his back.

Chapter Fifteen

Drew gasped and shuddered as the cold liquid soaked through his shirt and dribbled down his spine.

"I'm sorry," Jessica apologized. She grabbed a dishcloth and stooped to mop up the spill.

"It's my fault for not being able to keep my hands off you," he teased. "I have towels and clean T-shirts folded on top of the dryer." He tugged the hem of his shirt free, whisked it off and headed for the laundry room.

Jessica's breath caught in her throat as she watched Drew, his back to her, toss his shirt on top of the washer and reach for his fresh laundry.

"My goodness, Drew! What happened?" she asked, pointing to fading scars on his spine and ribs. She knew from experience the damage must have been substantial.

Drew turned and glanced down at his chest, also

marked with scar tissue. "Oh, that?" He waved it off nonchalantly. "Cut myself shaving."

"This is no time to joke. Come here and talk to me." She sank onto his leather sofa and patted the seat next to her. "Those look several years older than mine."

"That's because it's been several years since the accident." He dragged a white shirt over his head and made himself comfortable beside her.

"You were in an accident?" Her voice rose. She took his hand and settled in to hear the story.

"I was part of an air assault team trained for crisis missions in Eastern Europe. We were practicing a HALO operation in the Italian Alps."

Jessica's eyes narrowed. "Halo? You mean like an angel's halo?"

He smiled at the common question. "No. HALO stands for high altitude, low opening."

"I'm sorry." She shook her head. "I've never heard the term."

"That's okay—most people have no idea it's possible, much less commonplace. A SEAL team pioneered the operation years ago and I've done it hundreds of times." He raked his hand through his hair.

"A transport plane dropped me from forty thousand feet. You wear a thermal suit and mask along with an oxygen bottle. At that altitude the temperature is subzero and it's common for your goggles to shatter and your eyes to freeze shut. But the greatest danger is from hypoxia, or lack of oxygen. A man can lose consciousness in an instant, so there's a pressure-activated rip cord to pop the chute if you don't.''

Her eyes flew open with disbelief and he hurried on.

''At close to three hundred miles an hour, you free-fall for a minute or so below radar cover before deploying the parachute. Since my team members were weapons experts, we each carried pieces of a portable tactical nuclear device that could be reassembled and armed very quickly on the ground.''

''A portable what?'' Her eyebrows scrunched together.

''A twenty-five megaton bomb.''

Jessica's expressive face began to register the incredulous look he'd come to anticipate when describing HALO operations.

''You're not serious,'' she insisted, leaning closer, studying him for signs of teasing. ''You *are* serious. Is that how you got hurt? Setting off a bomb?'' Her green eyes got wider by the moment.

''I never got that far.'' He sucked in a deep breath and blew it out loudly. ''At one thousand feet the chute automatically deploys. A charge fires into the canopy, to blast it open immediately, so you'll decelerate in time to survive the landing.''

Drew would never forget the absolute terror of the moment.

''Something went wrong. The charge never fired.

My chute slowed me, but not nearly enough. I hit the ground at sixty miles an hour.''

Jessica grimaced and shifted on the cushion. She sat facing him, cross-legged, her knees pressed against his thigh.

"Drew, it's a miracle you're alive."

"It was one of many miracles God performed that day," he assured her. "I was thrown off target, so I fell on an incline instead of flat ground. I glanced off the frozen mountainside and rolled downhill. That's the only thing that saved me from being crushed."

Her hand slid to his shoulder where she gently stroked the back of his neck. He smiled his gratitude for the comforting touch and patted her hand.

"How badly were you hurt?" From the knowing expression in her eyes, the light of understanding was dawning.

"Well, let's see." He ticked off the injuries matter-of-factly. "My neck was broken, my spine was ruptured in several places, the left femur was shattered and my right kneecap had been completely ripped off. My lung was punctured and I can't remember how many ribs were broken. Throw in a nasty head gash and it's no wonder I was temporarily blind and had a ruptured eardrum." He smiled sheepishly. "Hence the loud music."

"You say you were in the Italian Alps when this happened." She kept shaking her head, amazed.

"That's another miracle. My team, God bless those guys, managed to find me within two hours. Otherwise, I'd have died from exposure.'' He hurried through the rest of the story. ''I really don't remember much about my hospitalization in Europe. It took weeks to stabilize me enough to move me back to the States. I had surgery at Walter Reed so many times I lost count. I spent months in sweaty, itchy body casts.'' He shuddered at the thought. ''That was a picnic compared to the physical therapy.''

''Please stop.'' Jessica held up a hand, fingers spread wide. ''Knowing you endured all that is too much to handle in one sitting.''

He grasped her hand, cupping it warmly.

''I understand that it's hard for you to hear. But believe it or not, that accident was the best thing that could have happened to me.''

She glared at him as if he'd just sprouted a third eye.

''How can you say that?''

''Because the agony of recovery and the bitterness over losing my career were more than I could bear on my own. One late night, alone in the hospital room, I just didn't want to go on. I gave my life and my pain to Christ. I pleaded with Him to heal my body and spirit or end my suffering. And I promised, at that moment, that either way, He would be in control.''

''I feel like such a selfish wimp for crying about my injury after what you've been through.''

''Don't. I cried loud and long. Many times.''

''Did you ever consider counseling?''

He laughed. "Are you kidding? I must have spent a thousand hours on the couch. The counseling brought on the crying. It's amazing how much progress everyone thinks you're making once you completely fall apart."

He scrunched his dark eyebrows at the memory.

"That's when I refused to let my father demand an investigation into the accident. I've accepted any responsibility that I may have for what happened. I'd packed my own equipment just like I'd done hundreds of times before. Maybe I was distracted. Maybe I did something differently. I don't know, and I'm not going to waste any more time trying to figure it out, because it won't change things."

She envied the glow of peace in Drew's eyes. She wondered how long it would be before she, too, could accept the way she'd been judged, always afraid that somehow she might have been even remotely responsible for the death of another human being.

"The more I get to know you, the more amazed I am that we have so much in common."

He leaned back, studying her face, his large hand trailing down her hair to her shoulder and arm.

"I'm glad to hear you say that. I was afraid you might not realize it."

She shivered at his light touch and buffed her palms over her forearms against the momentary chill.

"Come on, let's get you home."

He stood, pulling her to her feet as the phone jangled.

"Hello?" He broke into a smile. "Hey, cutie pie! How are you?"

Jessica followed his movements as he turned away. He busied himself clearing off the counter, moving the few items from the sink to the dishwasher.

He listened patiently, asking questions about Faith's friends. His interest in their activities made Jessica's heart glow with warmth.

Remembering his incredible story, Jessica felt a shudder skitter through her body. God had spared Drew and brought him into her life. To love.

There was no denying it. She loved him. But could he ever return her feelings?

And if he could, would his father accept their relationship?

"I'll be home in a few months and, yes, you can wait that long." He paused, smiling at Jessica. "Okay, I'll be sure to do that. When Father returns from his trip give him my love. Bye."

He'd hardly laid the phone back in its cradle when it rang again. He snatched it back up with a smile and punched the talk button. "Of course, I love you, too," he greeted the caller.

"Well, I'm certainly glad to see that you've come to your senses." The sultry voice floated over the line.

"Amelia." He glanced at Jessica as he spoke. "What do you want?"

Jessica turned to leave. He quickly motioned her to sit down and he held up one finger to ask for a little time. Then he turned away so she wouldn't have to hear.

"Please, Drew, we can't let this misunderstanding upset our plans. I've finally found a man Daddy approves of. He'll be furious if he thinks I've spoiled our future together."

"We don't have anything together."

"That's not true. Don't let a little difference of opinion get in the way of the good we can do for the people of this state."

He was silent, turning just in time to see his front door close quietly behind Jessica. He let out a deep sigh of resignation. It wasn't lost on Amelia.

"Just come listen to me for five minutes. That's all I ask."

He had to admit this was entirely his fault. The least he could do was apologize properly.

"Okay. I'll be at your place at eight in the morning."

Drew went out and knocked lightly on Jessica's door. He waited impatiently in the hallway as Frasier's anxious barking ceased and a single pair of footsteps approached the door. Darkness swallowed up the tiny beam of light behind the peephole and the dead bolt turned.

Jessica's face was scrubbed pink and her hair was braided. She wore a T-shirt and flannel pajama bottoms.

Drew thought he'd never seen anything so appealing in his life.

He sensed her fear even before she spoke.

"You're going to see Amelia."

His gut twisted at the statement of the fait accompli, and he wished he could correct her.

"Believe it or not, Amelia also had a lot riding on our relationship, and ending it is complicated."

"But it would be simple to end things with me." She stepped back, putting distance between them. His hand shot out, catching her chin and pulling her back to face him.

"Come on, Jess. I didn't say that."

"Drew, you have enough complications in your life. We both do. Maybe it's best if we settle for friendship."

"It's way too late for that." He slipped his hand away from her chin and slid it around the back of her neck. With his other hand he reached behind her waist as he stepped closer. He bent his head to hers and captured her mouth.

Her hands moved up the length of his back, and for endless moments they clung together.

Jessica braced her palms against his chest and gently pushed away, breaking the kiss. Her eyes were too shiny when she looked up at him.

"Go do your talking."

She stepped back across the safety of the threshold and prepared to close the door.

"First I need to say one thing to you," he insisted.

She held her breath. He could see she expected the worst.

"I love you, Jess," he whispered hoarsely.

In a déjà vu moment he puckered his lips, blew her a noisy kiss and was gone.

The tall man paid the cabdriver and rushed through the familiar airport. He passed the security checkpoint and stepped onto a waiting transport bus in time to make the final flight of the day.

He handed the unnecessary identification to the congenial gate agent.

"Courtesy seating has already begun, so you may board at your convenience, Senator Keegan."

Marcus Keegan nodded in response and hurried on.

Chapter Sixteen

Five-thirty. The novelty clock built from a '65 automobile hubcap, hanging over his stereo, stared back at him. Drew had invited Jessica to meet him at the High Museum at seven o'clock, after her appointment with a new client. He wanted to blurt out the details of his meeting with Amelia, but it was something that deserved to be said face-to-face. He knew from the look of resignation in Jessica's eyes last night, and the sound of her voice today, that his proposal would be a surprise.

He lifted the small velvet box and snapped open the lid for the tenth time that hour. It wasn't the family heirloom he'd always hoped to give his bride, but the two-carat oval diamond, which had cost him restoration services on a Boss 302, would certainly be worn with pride. Jessica was blessedly far from petite, and no small engagement stone would do.

He leaned his head back against soft sofa cushions and as he closed his eyes in an effort to relax and pray his mother's face filled his mind's eye. Over a decade had passed since her death, but no picture was needed to remind him of her beauty or her spirit.

"Oh, Mom, I know you'd love her," he whispered aloud. "She's so determined to do things on her own. Even if she doesn't need my help, I hope she needs my love."

The intercom buzzer jolted him off the couch and toward the speaker by the front door.

"Drew Keegan here."

"Son?"

"Sir!"

"If you'll clear me, I'll be in your parking lot in ten seconds."

Drew activated the gates and slid the velvet box into his pocket. Self-consciously he confirmed his shirt was neatly tucked. He glanced down the length of his creased jeans and wished for another sixty seconds to change into his leather loafers. Sneakers would have to do.

By the time he reached the vestibule and swung open the heavy door, his father's rental car was pulling alongside the curb.

"Faith said you were traveling. Is everything okay?"

Marcus stepped from the conservative sedan and reached for his son. The two men clasped hands and drew one another into a hug.

"With such a big decision hanging in the balance, I just couldn't leave things the way we did."

Drew warmed with embarrassment for the way he'd abruptly ended their last conversation. Seeing his father here in Atlanta, Drew felt his heart clutch. There was still a chance Marcus might see things from Drew's perspective.

"Thank you for coming, sir."

Marcus glanced toward the copper dome of the Commons and nodded his approval.

"Quite a nice place you have here."

Drew recalled his first impression of Sacred Arms and offered his father the same tour of the gardens that Valentine had given that first day. Drew painstakingly pointed out the many improvements that had been made to the grounds in recent years. Although he avoided mentioning Jessica by name, his message was clear from the many references to the landscape design artist.

Marcus admired the grounds, but he never once let Drew finish a statement about Jessica. It became painfully obvious he hadn't softened to the idea that a future with a glorified gardener, no matter how talented, was the right future for his only son.

They climbed the fieldstone path in silence. Drew realized they could hardly be further apart on the subject.

The metal door banged closed behind them as they entered the quiet hallway. Drew reached for his keys as he passed Jessica's door. He brushed two fingers over the velvet box in his pocket. His heart thumped hard.

He opened the front door and stepped aside respectfully.

"It won't take long for me to make us some coffee, sir. You have a look around."

The two exchanged comments on the architecture and restoration of the building. Drew ground aromatic beans and added bottled springwater to the coffee-maker. While the pool of dark brew collected in the glass pot, Drew waited for his father to get to the point of his visit.

"You have a beautiful home," Marcus said as he returned from inspecting the rooms upstairs. "Now I know where your sister's gotten the idea for a new bathtub."

Drew glanced at the kitchen clock. He'd planned to leave at six. He was already ten minutes late and he needed to change.

Marcus took the proffered cup. He kept his eyes down, stirring his coffee.

"I know you have plans for the evening, son, and I'm sorry if I'm holding you up." He fixed his eyes on Drew. "But I just can't allow you to commit to such a poorly thought out decision."

Drew gripped the counter's edge to steady himself while he searched for the right words.

"Sir, while your approval means a great deal to me, I'm not looking for your permission. This isn't just about me. It's about Jessica and me and how we feel about each other.''

"Oh, I don't doubt you have feelings for the woman. But, Andrew, you don't make life-changing decisions based upon feelings. You make them based upon facts. And if I understand correctly, the facts are that this woman's past, not to mention her present, makes her completely inappropriate for you to consider as a wife. I implore you to give this more time. Don't deal yourself a setback you may regret the rest of your life.''

Anger churned in Drew's center. Afraid he was about to damage the relationship with his father beyond repair, Drew motioned for Marcus to follow him to the sofa.

Holy Father, give me the words to get through to him, Drew prayed silently.

When both men were seated, he leaned forward, moved the worn Bible aside and opened the mahogany chest he kept on the tabletop. He gently withdrew a letter postmarked during his freshman year at West Point.

"Don't ask me why, but of all the letters Mom sent to me at school, I kept this one. I read it once in a while to feel close to her and to help remind me of the way Faith used to be.'' He placed the letter in his father's outstretched hand and stood. "I'm sorry to cut our visit so short, but I'm meeting Jessica this evening. Please make yourself comfortable while I change.''

* * *

Marcus held the letter tenderly, eyes misting at the sight of the familiar handwriting. He carefully opened the flap and withdrew the pages of embossed stationery.

Dear Andrew,

Today has been one of those crazy days for your father and me. One minute we were poring over brochures for a summer vacation and the next he was packing for a special session and I was cooking a pot roast for a member of our church who suddenly lost her husband. Your father's quick departure and this unexpected death have got me down. I thought maybe spending a few minutes with you might help.

For some time now it's been in my heart to tell you how proud you've made me. You've grown into such a marvelous young man with a tremendous sense of service and leadership. You get those things from Marcus. Heaven knows that if it were left up to me I'd hardly give blood, much less so much of my time and energy. You know I never planned on living a public life. Your father's ambition changed everything, and somehow I've managed to adapt. But if it weren't for our love and total commitment to one another I don't believe I could have handled all of this.

Now I've probably said too much. But you're

a grown man, Andrew, and I don't want to pass up this opportunity to give you some sage advice. Your choice of a mate is the most important decision you'll ever make. If love isn't at the center of the relationship, it cannot survive. A marriage can falter under the best of conditions, so when it's stressed to its limits, it had better have a solid foundation to support it through the tough times.

For me that foundation has always been our family. Loving the three of you fiercely, and wanting whatever's best for my children, has kept me sane on days when one more fund-raiser or toll booth dedication would otherwise have driven me over the edge. I look forward to the day when we retire from the Senate and life is our own again, if that's ever truly possible. Hopefully, you and Faith will give us a houseful of noisy grandchildren to spoil rotten in our golden years.

Speaking of Faith, your sister is a constant source of amazement. Last month she thought managing her own restaurant would be just the thing and this week she's passionate about going to law school so she can become a judge. She told me in no uncertain terms that she's a woman with a limitless future and that I'm holding her back by not allowing her to drive yet. I swear you were never this headstrong at thirteen!

Well, I am feeling better now. I should probably just throw this letter away and consider the time writing it as therapy. But I'd never want to pass up the chance to tell my son how much I love him and miss his company. The music room is too quiet without you.

Love, Mom

Marcus read the letter several times. Fingering the pages softly, he lifted them to his face and inhaled, somehow expecting to find her scent still clinging. How like her to unknowingly leave behind words of wisdom and comfort. How like Andrew to treasure them and use them now, to give the same wisdom and comfort to his opinionated father.

He glanced at the watch that was his Senate retirement gift and knew it would be a waste of time to delay Andrew a moment longer. He was clearly on a mission.

Folding the letter carefully back into its envelope, Marcus gently returned it to the keepsake box. When the mahogany box was once again centered exactly in the middle of the table, he reached into his breast pocket and deposited a treasure of his own atop the old family Bible. He took one last approving look at the very organized surroundings and headed toward the door.

Escaping the noise of Peachtree Street, Jessica stepped into the hushed quiet of Atlanta's favorite gallery. She felt pressure on her chest, the same weight of despair that she experienced in the old familiar dream. She buffed her palms over her forearms to fight off the chilling feeling.

She crossed the heart-of-pine floor and moved deeper into the cool museum, aware of the extraordinary collection of photographs on display, but not taking the time to appreciate them. Stopping before a collection on loan from a benevolent rock star, she checked her appearance in the glare from the glass of a life-size portrait.

Not surprisingly, her collar was turned up on one side, her lipstick was long since chewed off and the clip she'd spent ten minutes arranging in her hair had slipped out somewhere between home and the museum's parking lot.

"Jessica?"

She turned toward the voice. Madeline Shure approached with her usual air of self-confidence, heels clicking rhythmically on the wood, face shaded by a thousand-dollar panama hat. Jessica bent to take the older woman's hand and they exchanged air kisses, the only kind Madeline ever participated in.

"I left you a phone message earlier, my dear. I insist you drop by for brunch tomorrow. I've invited several friends who've shown interest in your services as well as in supporting Helping Hands. If you have a final statement, bring that along and we'll settle up."

Remembering the substantial bill that was still outstanding, Jessica quickly agreed. She needed to pay the mortgage and make good on her deal with Sam.

"You've been so generous, I don't know how I'll ever thank you."

"Nonsense." Madeline waved the gratitude aside. "You helped me pull off a spectacular event and I won't soon forget it. Now I have to run. There's a small gathering in one of the private rooms in the back. Some sort of surprise announcement and I can't be late." She touched the brim of her hat.

Jessica stood alone for a while as a number of familiar faces hurried past. One couple recognized her and politely nodded their acknowledgment, while another pretended not to notice her at all.

Flushing at the obvious snubbing, she turned away from the oncoming traffic and stared through the glass wall at the lengthening shadows outside. It had to be getting close to eight. She squinted her eyes impatiently and searched for Drew among the pedestrians.

When she spotted his powerfully broad shoulders, a shard of anxiety lodged in her chest. She pressed her hand against her heart and felt its erratic beat. Turning away before he could see her reaction, she closed her eyes and practiced a long-neglected relaxation technique. It was a waste of time.

She caught his reflection in the darkening glass as he entered the museum and crossed the room. Her heart pounded harder at the smile that played across his face. When he reached for her she turned quickly, jumping to avoid his touch.

"I'm sorry," he apologized. "I didn't mean to startle you."

"It's okay." She brought her hand to her heart once more.

"I'm also sorry for being so late. I got held up and I was determined to take the time to change." He motioned toward his clothes. She drank in the sight of his beloved in a navy suit and monogrammed dress shirt.

He continued, "I knew you'd dress for the evening—and you're amazing in that color."

Immediately self-conscious, she smoothed her hands down the front of her new green jacket and matching silk slacks, another of Becky Jo's selections that she claimed was the perfect complement to her friend's figure.

Drew leaned in and growled seductively into her ear.

She swatted him away and glanced around to see if anybody had heard. He took her hand and began to tug her along behind him, seemingly in search of some privacy. At the end of the hallway, a wooden bench was fitted into an alcove. With the bench in their sights, he slowed.

Excitement buzzed in a nearby room, but she tuned it out as they stood close together. Drew took her hand and threaded her fingers through his. He sucked in a deep breath. As he opened his mouth to begin, she quickly interrupted.

"So did you and Amelia set a date?"

His jaw snapped shut and the look in his eyes changed from anticipation to a confusing calm.

"Do you honestly think that's a reasonable question?"

She pretended to mull it over.

"Hmm, if I remember correctly, we were interrupted last night by a phone call from your former girlfriend and you made an appointment to see her first thing this morning. Considering who we're dealing with here, I'd say it's quite reasonable."

"In that case, let me give you a reality check. Right after she admitted she'd complained to Daniel Ellis, I told Amelia, for the *last* time, that there could never have been anything between us because I'm in love with you, Jessica Holliday."

"You said that to her?" Jessica was breathless from the revelation.

"Word for word."

He pulled her into his arms, tipping her face up to his. Clutching her tightly with one hand, he used the other to softly caress her cheek.

He sat and drew her down to the bench beside him. When she was seated, he turned and went down on one knee, taking both her hands in his.

"Jess..." His voice became hoarse with emotion. "Last night I told you I love you, and it was the first time I've ever said that to a woman." He raised her hands to his lips.

"I'm thirty-two years old and I've never felt this before. My heart pounds when you walk into the room and when you leave my sight there is honest-to-goodness pain. And I'm a man who knows something about pain.'' He gazed deeply into her eyes.

''When you laugh with me, I feel a peace I can't even understand. And when you let me help you, it gives me as much satisfaction as any job of my own ever has.'' He choked to nothing more than a whisper.

''There's a specific reason I wanted to meet you here tonight.'' He regarded the masterful works of art that graced the walls and then squeezed Jessica's hands tightly. ''I needed a place filled with priceless beauty to ask a timeless beauty an important question. Do you love me?''

The lump in her throat made it impossible to speak. The exquisite fear in her heart only moments earlier had been replaced by a sweet peace that comes only from the experience of God's handiwork. Hearing Drew's confession of love was more than she'd ever dared to hope for. To pray for.

She nodded her head, sending unshed tears trickling over her lashes. Drew brushed his fingertips gently over her cheeks.

''That's all the answer I need. Jessica Holliday, I love you. Will you marry me?'' he pleaded. ''Please.''

Chapter Seventeen

Before Jessica could speak, the double doors across the hall burst open. She recognized members of the press, who exited quickly, clearly intent on making air and print deadlines.

Drew was waiting for her answer, but she was struck dumb by the commotion of what happened next. Raymond Crockett strolled through the doorway, a self-satisfied smile on his face. When he spotted the two in the alcove, his pleasant mood appeared to dissolve. He stopped dead still, eyes darting to the left where the press had left the building, and then crossed the hall to stand before them. Jessica felt the warmth drain from her face.

Still kneeling, Drew turned at the sound of footsteps behind him. He stood, his body a barrier between her and Crockett.

"It's okay, Drew. I can handle this myself." She

stepped out from behind him and faced Adam's father.

She could tell his rage was barely contained.

"I can't believe either of you had the nerve to show up here today," he hissed through clenched teeth.

Jessica's spine stiffened.

"Mr. Crockett, I had no idea you'd be here. But even if I had, I wouldn't have avoided you."

"But I bet you'd both have avoided *me*."

Draped in a conservative black dress, Amelia emerged on the arm of eligible bachelor and city councilman Richard "Bubba" Estes. With her scrawny arm linked through Bubba's, she reminded Jessica of a black widow latched on to her latest victim.

"Why would either of us do that, Amelia?" Drew spoke before Jessica had a chance.

Amelia smiled and licked her lips as her gaze darted from Jessica to Drew and back to her father again.

"Our wedding announcement will be on the eleven o'clock news tonight." She and her city councilman headed toward the stretch limo waiting at the curb.

"I don't get you, Keegan." Raymond Crockett's jaw was tense. "They said you had brass and big ambition like your old man. You had the target in your sights. All you had to do was pull the trigger." He turned to walk away and then threw one last shot over his shoulder.

"Tell Marcus that thanks to Jessica Holliday you

were finished in the South before you ever got started.''

''Sir, if Jessica and I decide that public service is in our future, there's nothing you can do to stop us.''

Crockett spun back around. Jessica was aware of how much he resembled his late son.

''Don't be too sure of that.'' He glared hatefully from one to the other. ''Either of you.''

Without another word he crossed the floor to the main entrance and joined his daughter in the limo.

Drew watched the retreating form of the man who'd just declared himself the enemy. He slipped one hand into his jacket and reached for Jessica with the other. She hesitated before placing a trembling hand into his. He pulled a magnificent diamond, mounted on a platinum band, from his pocket and slid it on Jessica's finger.

''Will you marry me?'' he repeated.

''You can't do this,'' she whispered.

''I can't do anything else,'' he insisted. ''My heart is yours, Jess. Completely. I want you to share my life.''

''What about your political career?''

''We're young. We have thirty years to work on that.''

''Drew, I know how your father feels about me.''

''Is that so?'' He raised the ring to his lips and kissed it lightly. ''This was my mother's ring. Father delivered it to me himself. We may have some work to do with him, but we're starting off with his blessing."

Jessica closed her eyes and leaned her forehead against Drew's chest. He folded her in his arms as she prayed silently.

Lord, You've overwhelmed me with answered prayer. This moment, I give You my heart and my commitment to love Andrew and his family till death parts us.

Tilting her head, she was drawn into the depths of brown eyes brimming with tears of love.

"No matter what happens in the future, Jess—family, finances, professions, health or reputation—no matter what comes our way…"

He kissed her softly, a sweet taste of the future.

"I promise we'll see it through together. Now, will you do me the honor of becoming my wife?"

"I can't do anything else." She mirrored his words. "My heart is yours, Andrew. Completely."

* * * * *

Dear Reader,

Five years ago I was amazed by the true story of a Green Beret's survival after dropping 40,000 feet with a defective parachute. I was compelled to spin a tale around this real-life hero and I wanted to create an equally special heroine for him. A woman with a real-life body and all the real-life fears that go along with it. Picture me getting started: a laptop on my bathroom counter, my faithful dog draped across my lap. After two years of watching me spend my weekends in the bathroom, my very own handsome hero transformed a closet into a workspace, and I became a "real writer."

My self-imposed rule was not to write anything that would offend my mother or my daughter. Try as I might, I couldn't ignore the call to do more, to use my words to glorify our Heavenly Father. *Hearts in Bloom* is my debut Love Inspired novel. I hope spending time with Jessica and Drew blesses you as much as writing their story has blessed me. Share your thoughts when you visit me at maenunn.com.

Until next time, let your light shine.

Mae Nunn

Love Inspired

A TIME TO REMEMBER

BY

LOIS RICHER

Grayson McGonigle's world had fallen apart the day his wife and son vanished. But five months later, a traumatized Marissa and Cody reappear, unable to speak about their harrowing ordeal. Can Gray help Marissa regain her memories of their happy married life…and build a love she can never forget?

Don't miss

A TIME TO REMEMBER

on sale June 2004

Available at your favorite retail outlet.

Love Inspired

LOVE COMES HOME

BY

TERRI REED

Rachel Maguire had always been sure of God's plan for her—a career in medicine to improve hospital conditions. That meant giving up the only man she'd ever loved: Joshua Taylor. But twelve years after she'd turned down his proposal, he was back in her life, making her wonder: Did God's plan for her include Josh and his young son?

Don't miss

LOVE COMES HOME

on sale June 2004

Available at your favorite retail outlet.

LILCH